JOURNEYS BEYOND THE PEAKS

Lauren's *dark* Passage

A NOVEL

M.F. ERLER

Praise for Lauren's Dark Passage...

*"**A poignant tale saturated with redemption and honesty**, all while placing us in the shoes of a single mother. "Lauren's Dark Passage" uses realistic scenes to tell a woman's journey from bitterness and darkness to optimism and light. You'll find yourself cheering for the protagonist and wanting to see what happens next."*

—SIERRA ZEMKE
Member Montana Women Writers, and Footprints Christian Writers

*"As Lauren travels through her dark passage, she is overwhelmed with emotions all too familiar to our human condition. Will she be able to move on from personal heartache into the light of forgiveness? **A story of love, loss, and the strength of family**...with a surprise visit from Peaks Saga Series' characters.*

M.F. Erler adds dimension to the family tree she's developed in her previous novels: The Peaks Saga Series *and* Voices in the Past.*"*

—J.M. GOODISON
Author of Footprints in History

*"This novel **speaks to many pertinent issues of our time** with a solid message of hope."*

— KATE FRASER
Author and member of Authors of the Flathead and Montana Women Writers

"When divorced, single parent Lauren Parker is faced with an existential crisis in midlife, she must gather strength from deeply held Christian principles to sustain herself and her children during the ordeal. Mostly she must find the way to forgive perceived sins—her own and those of others. Her hope is that God will provide needed sustenance through her painful journey. In Lauren's Dark Passage *M.F. Erler has provided thoughtful insights for women faced with Lauren's dilemma. **It's a poignant read**."*

— BONNIE SMITH
Member of The Authors of the Flathead and Rocky Mountain Fiction Writers and published author of The Soul of Frannie Cooper *among others*

JOURNEYS BEYOND THE PEAKS

Standalones

VOICES IN THE PAST

LAUREN'S DARK PASSAGE

FAR FROM MAGNOLIA DRIVE

THE PEAKS SAGA

Series

PEAKS AT THE EDGE
OF THE WORLD - *Finding the Light*

SEARCHING FOR MAIA

MOUNTAINTOPS AND VALLEYS

WHEN THE WORLD GROWS COLD

THE FOUNTAIN AND THE DESERT

BEYOND THE WORLD

WHERE ALL WORLDS END

JOURNEYS BEYOND THE PEAKS

Lauren's *dark* Passage

A NOVEL

M.F. ERLER

LAUREN'S DARK PASSAGE, *Journeys Beyond the Peaks*
by M.F. Erler

Copyright © 2022 M.F. Erler
All Rights Reserved

First Edition April 2023

FIRST STEPS PUBLISHING
Gleneden Beach, Oregon
FirstStepsPublishing.com

ISBN:
   978-1-944072-76-6 (hc)
   978-1-944072-77-3 (pb)
   978-1-944072-78-0 (epub)

Cover photo by Paul Erler
Cover design and formatting by Suzanne Fyhrie Parrott

Please provide feedback

10 9 8 7 6 5 4 3 2 1

Printed in U.S.A.

While this book is a spinoff from the original characters developed in *The Peaks at the Edge of the World Saga*, it does not have to be read in any particular order with my other works. However, the events in this book do fall in the interlude between Peaks Saga Book 3 and Book 4. Ginna Parker, Lauren's daughter, is one of the main characters in all *The Peaks Saga* books. Annemarie Parker's story is found in *Books 4 & 5*.

DISCLAIMER: While the *Peaks Saga Series* is suitable for teens and adults, this book and others in *The Journeys Saga Series* are **_adult_** in content and tone.

DEDICATION

This book is dedicated to my husband, Paul
     –love of my life.
As we approach our 50th wedding anniversary,
I count my blessings that our marriage has
weathered the storms of life.
My heart aches that many others haven't.

"Two are better than one,
Because they have a good return for their work:
If one falls down, his friend can help him up!
Also, if two lie down together, they will keep warm,
But how can one keep warm alone?
Though one may be overpowered,
Two can defend themselves.
A cord of three strands is not quickly broken."
—Ecclesiastes 4:9-12

"I have told you these things, so that in me you may have
     peace.
In this world you will have trouble.
But take heart! I have overcome the world."
—John 16:33

ACKNOWLEDGEMENTS

The more I write, the more I realize it isn't a completely solo activity. I would not have completed this book without the help and suggestions of:

Paul Erler, Mary Schmidt, Bonnie Smith, Janice Goodison, Sierra Zemke, and Kate Fraser. I am most grateful to each of them.

The Parker / Evans Family Tree *(fictional)*

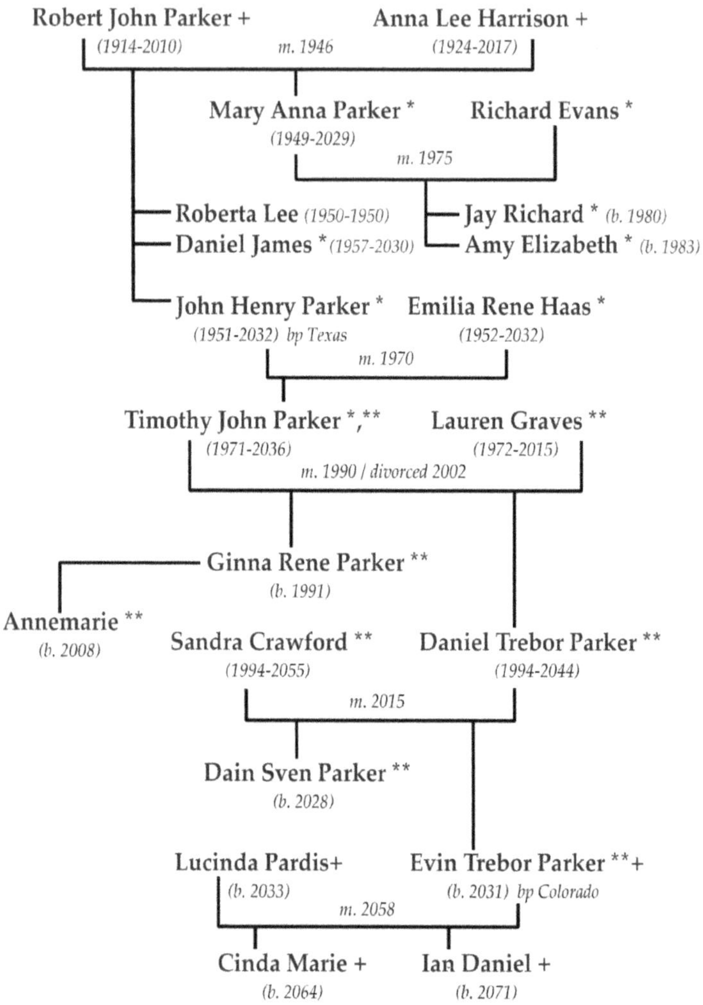

Robert John Parker + *(1914-2010)* — *m. 1946* — **Anna Lee Harrison +** *(1924-2017)*

Mary Anna Parker * *(1949-2029)* — *m. 1975* — **Richard Evans ***

- **Roberta Lee** *(1950-1950)*
- **Daniel James *** *(1957-2030)*
- **Jay Richard *** *(b. 1980)*
- **Amy Elizabeth *** *(b. 1983)*

John Henry Parker * *(1951-2032) bp Texas* — *m. 1970* — **Emilia Rene Haas *** *(1952-2032)*

Timothy John Parker *,** *(1971-2036)* — *m. 1990 / divorced 2002* — **Lauren Graves **** *(1972-2015)*

Ginna Rene Parker ** *(b. 1991)*

Annemarie ** *(b. 2008)*

Sandra Crawford ** *(1994-2055)* — *m. 2015* — **Daniel Trebor Parker **** *(1994-2044)*

Dain Sven Parker ** *(b. 2028)*

Lucinda Pardis+ *(b. 2033)* — *m. 2058* — **Evin Trebor Parker **+** *(b. 2031) bp Colorado*

Cinda Marie + *(b. 2064)* — **Ian Daniel +** *(b. 2071)*

Characters are in:

* *Far from Magnolia Drive*

** *The Peaks Saga* books

+ *Voices in the Past*

CHAPTER 1
No Man's Land

When I was young, my dad and I watched movies about World War I and II. He liked them, and I wanted to be with him, especially as his pancreatic cancer grew worse. Somehow the idea of watching scenes of people struggling courageously in battle must have helped him during his own ordeal.

"Life is a battle, Lauren," he often said. "Too many people expect it to be a peaceful picnic."

I was barely into my teens then, and the meaning of his words didn't sink in. But I liked how he took my hand when scenes in the movie were especially tense or gruesome.

"If you have a hand to hold, it helps," he'd say. "That's what the Good Lord does, holds your hand."

Now I remembered these words as the sun spilled into the hospital room the morning after my double mastectomy.

All my adult life, I'd known that cancer ran in my family. My mother's breast cancer had taken her life only two years after Dad died. Staring at the ceiling of my hospital room, I tried to draw strength and comfort from my father's words all those years ago. Instead, nothing but silence filled my mind.

"I know I should lean on you, Lord," I murmured aloud. "But I feel so alone. How can I find you?"

Yesterday, just before they took me into surgery, there had been a brief glimpse of light in my mind. Now I attempted to conjure it up again. Unfortunately, too many other thoughts flooded in, wiping that vision of light away. All that came was a fragment of scripture I'd heard somewhere: "In this world you will have trouble...."

So many things had happened in my forty years of life, and lying here so weak and in pain, all I could remember were the trials and heartaches.

Maybe if I let them flow over and through me, I might find some hope on the other side. I tried to think back on good times, but sleep overwhelmed me first.

With a painful jerk, I awoke from a dream about my dad. This time, we'd been watching *All Quiet on the Western Front,* a film about World War I. My mind had filled with images of acres of barbed wire, blasted land full of holes and pits from artillery shells, mud mingled with blood, bodies lying where no one could retrieve them—No Man's Land. So bleak, so fearful, such a waste of land and lives. And for what?

"Daddy, why does God allow people to have wars?" I'd asked that day.

"I don't know, Kitten," he sighed, using his pet name for me. He didn't say it as often now that I was a teenager, so I knew he felt especially sentimental that day.

"Why do they call it No Man's Land?" I added.

"Because no one can survive there. It's kind of like where I am now, somewhere between life and death."

He looked away as he said this, but I grabbed his hand. "Daddy, please don't die."

At that point in my dream, I woke, heart throbbing and chest aching. Had this scene happened in real life? It was so long ago; I couldn't be sure. Yet it was part of my psyche now, for I was in No Man's Land, too.

My father had died when I was fourteen, just about to enter high school. By this time, my mother had been diagnosed with breast cancer. The first mastectomy had revealed many affected lymph nodes, and Mom was dealing with the side effects of chemo while we tried to plan Dad's funeral. She was too overwhelmed to have more than just a simple graveside service. This left me bereft of support from friends and family, something I desperately needed. But there was no way to change it.

All I could do was start high school in Crockett, Texas. Some friends from my junior high were in my classes, but many were on different academic tracks. I felt abandoned and alone, lost in a crowd of strangers.

They diagnosed cancer in my mother's other breast by the time they evaluated the results of her first round of chemo. Dad had been gone a year already, but I still missed him so much that it hurt. Many nights, tears soaked my pillow. The doctors discussed another mastectomy for Mom, but cancer had spread to her lungs and stomach. Back in those days, there was nothing more they could do.

She died at the beginning of my senior year. I lost the house due to medical bills and was an only child. Where would I go?

Aunt Tammy, one of Dad's sisters in Crockett, took me in so I could finish in the same high school. I knew Tammy tried, but she was a rather solemn person who'd never raised any children of her own. Life became an emotional desert until I met Tim Parker during the spring of my senior year. He lived up the road in Palestine, not far away, so we went to each other's senior proms and other special events. Soon we were steady dates.

It's no surprise that he became my port in the storm. He was a gentle young man. So, with no one else in my world who loved or cared for me, it made perfect sense to get married shortly after graduation.

Those first years after high school had been the best part of my life. At least that was how it looked in hindsight from my hospital bed. We had married in 1990 and bought a little house in Rusk, Texas—only an hour from his family home in Palestine. Soon we had a daughter, Ginna, and three years later, a son, Danny. Tim had been an attentive father, and I accepted that sexual passion wasn't something important to him. But once the children were born, things began to unravel bit by bit, though, at first, I ignored the signs.

First, Tim began working late most evenings. Then, every month or so, he had to travel for meetings. I'd asked one time for details about these trips, and he'd blown up.

"It's none of your business," he'd snapped. "I do what my work requires, and you take care of the house and kids. That's your job."

I was speechless at this outburst. He'd never talked like this before. "Wait, I thought we had a partnership here. I want to be your helper, your mate. We're not just roommates, living our own separate lives."

Now I don't remember how he replied. All my mind's eye conjures is the image of his stomping toward the back door. My husband had always been a kind, even-tempered man. "What have I done wrong?" I called to his retreating back. "I just want to know where to reach you in case of an emergency."

"You can call my office for that, Lauren."

"But what if it's the middle of the night?"

"Then you manage it yourself." He slammed the door and headed for the garage.

After this exchange, I drew away from him. He was becoming a stranger to me, not at all like the man I'd married.

After several months of this, he stormed into the house one day after working late again. Danny and Ginna were already upstairs in their bedrooms, tucked in for the night. Before I could say a word, he slammed a stack of papers on the kitchen counter.

"I want a divorce," was all he said. His eyes were avoiding mine, and his voice sounded distant.

"W-what?" I'd had no warning that something like this was coming.

"I've found someone else," he snapped. "This just isn't working for me anymore."

This was the first time since my parents' deaths that I felt that old darkness and emptiness rising in my body and soul.

"Why can't we keep going to counseling, Tim? Things seemed to be getting better."

We had been seeing a marriage counselor for about six months, but sometimes Tim begged off going, saying he had too much work to do.

"I've had enough of that wasted time. Nothing is going to change for me."

"Why not?"

"Because I'm gay," he snapped. "I want to live with my partner, Michael."

The room spun around me, and I grabbed the edge of the countertop to keep from falling.

"You can't mean that! How can you do this to us?"

"I never should have married you, Lauren. I guess I thought it might cure me if I tried living a normal life with a wife and kids. But it's not working."

I sank onto one of the barstools at the breakfast bar, vertigo still whirling. "I don't believe you, Tim. What is your lover's real name?"

"I've told you the truth." He turned on his heel and stomped out the back door.

The next time we were in the same room together was in divorce court. Thinking back, there's a huge blank spot in my memory. How did I tell Danny and Ginna? I can remember saying that their father was leaving for someone he loved more. I couldn't bring myself to tell them Tim said he was gay. Ginna was barely ten, and Danny was seven.

By this time, the years had rolled into 2002. More and more people were proclaiming the need for Gay Rights, but my conservative religious upbringing shrank back from accepting all this. Finally, after the divorce was final, Tim sent a letter trying to defend himself.

"I can't help who I am," he'd written. "All I can do is be true to myself."

But my mind recoiled. I wasn't ready to see his point of view. Once I tried to reply to his letter, but couldn't find any words to say. So instead, I burned the letter along with my attempted answer in an ashtray I bought at a thrift store—wishing we had a fireplace for the job.

The divorce gave him our house, and I got the rest of the belongings—and the children. Child custody went to me, and he was to provide child support monthly. We were going to work out his visitation rights once I knew where I would live. I couldn't face telling any of my friends the truth about the situation. All I wanted was to get out of Rusk—out of Texas altogether. I had no family to turn to, no siblings. My in-laws were only an hour away, but this felt awkward rather than helpful.

***

As my mind rolled on in that hospital bed, I realized my in-laws had always struck me as an odd couple. Tim's father, John, was so quiet that I'd rarely heard him speak, while his mother, Emilia, was more outspoken. She often bragged to me about how she'd raised her two sons to be "just about perfect." It didn't take long for this to become advice on how to bring up Danny. Even before Tim left, I'd found my mother-in-law's presence overwhelming.

After the divorce, Emilia became quieter, but was this just showing her disapproval? Soon, however, she began calling frequently, asking when I was going to bring Ginna and Danny over to see them. I put her off as long as I could, afraid Emilia would fill the kids with negative ideas about me.

The Parkers had all grown up in East Texas and weren't scattered far from their roots. John's family still lived close to their hometown of Palestine.

In keeping with family tradition, Tim and I had lived nearby in Rusk. This small town was originally a stop on the tiny East Texas Railroad. The line was still used for tourism, with a little antique steam train running back and forth between Rusk and Palestine.

A couple of months after the divorce was finalized, I gave in and agreed to meet Emilia at the Rusk station and put the kids on the train with her. That way, they could ride up to their grandparents', visit for a night, and come back by train the next day. Danny, who loved trains, was jubilant. Since it was close to his ninth birthday, the outing could take the place of the birthday party I couldn't afford—especially since Emilia was paying for the trip.

Emilia waved from a small platform on the first car when the locomotive came puffing into the station, her long blonde hair blowing in the breeze. I kept my focus on my kids as they waved back. Ginna seemed less enthusiastic about this whole arrangement than Danny, but then she was almost thirteen and wanted to present herself as what she pictured an adult should be.

"There's Grandma," I murmured, unable to think of anything else to say.

The engine let off a blast of steam, an ear-splitting whistle blew, and the train finally creaked and clanged to a stop beside the platform. "Go ahead," I urged the kids. "Meet Grandma at the ticket booth so you can get good seats for the ride back."

"I guess we have to," Ginna shrugged. "You'll be here tomorrow when we come back, right Mom?"

"Of course, I will. I don't have anything else to do." This was before I'd found a job. Even though Tim was getting the house, he wasn't forcing us to move out yet.

Ginna gave me a side glance I couldn't decipher and took her brother's hand. "Come on, Danny. We have to do this."

"I'm going to love it," he babbled. "Just look at the smoke from the engine. This is so cool."

While they were in line, the engine unhooked and moved into a little roundhouse just past the depot. There it was turned and reemerged, heading in the opposite direction. Then it chugged up a siding until it was at the other end of the cars, ready to pull them back to Palestine.

Once Emilia bought the tickets, she came over to where I sat on one of the wooden benches under the station's overhanging roof. "Thank you, Lauren," she smiled. "We're going to take the kids out for pizza tonight."

"Yeah, I love pizza," piped Danny.

Ginna just nodded, looking at the ground. Was she still putting on her cool teenager act?

"Maybe Dairy Queen for dessert," added Emilia.

Ginna did look up at this. I knew how much my daughter liked ice cream and gave her a quick smile, trying to telepathically send her the message that the whole experience wouldn't be so bad.

The train whistle shrilled again, saving me from thinking of something to say. Giving the kids quick hugs, I watched them follow their grandmother up the steps into one of the vintage coaches. Soon they were waving through the window as the train pulled away.

***

The next day, they waved and grinned as the train pulled into the Rusk Depot. I heaved a sigh of relief. The visit must have gone well. Both kids were talking at once when they rushed up to me.

"We had a huge pepperoni pizza," Danny was saying. "I ate four pieces."

"I got to have a chocolate-chip cookie dough blizzard," Ginna said simultaneously.

"Hey, one at a time," I laughed.

"I hope I didn't spoil them too much," Emilia said as she came up behind me. I ground my teeth and managed not to seem startled.

"Oh, well," I smiled. "They'll get a good dose of reality soon enough. Life with a single mom can be tight financially."

Emilia frowned and looked away.

I knew I shouldn't have said that, insinuating Tim was at fault, but it came out anyway.

"So what are your plans, Lauren?"

Now I heard the bite in her voice.

"I've been job-hunting on the Internet," I replied. "Something will come up soon, and then we can move out of Tim's house."

"Ah," was all Emilia said. "Well, I do hope Ginna and Danny can come visit again soon."

I forced a smile while my kids beamed at me.

"Yes, Mom," said Danny. "We loved it."

I probably would have let them go again, but I found the Colorado job about a month later. After the children were in bed, I'd spent all my evenings searching the Internet. The job was as a public relations assistant for a nuclear power plant in eastern Colorado. I had just enough computer and keyboarding skills to qualify.

Even though the kids were disappointed to move away from their grandparents, I was determined to make my own way without relying on a husband or in-laws.

If my parents had still been living, I could have counted on them, but both of them were gone. This early taste of heartbreak had forced me into more independence, but it helped a lot now as I made my way into uncharted territory.

After moving to Colorado, the kids and I just tried to make it from day to day. They were unhappy in Deer Path since it was much smaller than Rusk. Kids at school teased about their southern accents. Being newcomers in a small rural school, where the students had known each other since kindergarten, left them isolated.

Emilia called often at first. Sometimes talking to her was almost pleasant, but my mother-in-law tended to load on unsolicited advice on the art of raising boys. She'd say, "I hope you can do as well with Danny as I did with Tim and Tony. It's just a shame that Tim isn't in your picture anymore. A boy needs a father figure."

"Tim could still do that if he wanted to," I retorted. "We have a visitation rights agreement, but he doesn't ever call. It's like he's erased his own children from his life."

"Well, he's still adjusting," she responded.

"So are we." I rolled my eyes, thankful Emilia couldn't see this over the phone. "For one thing, he's delinquent on his child-support payments."

"You're just too impatient, Lauren. Things will come together soon."

Of course, Emilia couldn't help making excuses for her dear boy, but I was so exasperated one day that I blurted out, "If you're such an expert on raising boys, why is your eldest son gay?"

Silence echoed over the phone line. "What a terrible thing to say," Emilia finally muttered. "You said it just to hurt me, didn't you? What have I ever done to deserve this?"

The line clicked, and she was gone.

Emilia never called again, which was what I probably had secretly wished. Still, I was telling the truth about my ex. He'd told me that he was leaving, not for another woman, but a man. I doubted he would have made that story up.

It was a month before I received another call from my in-laws' number. I almost didn't answer but was thankful I did when I heard John's voice on the line.

"Lauren, is it true what you told Emilia about Tim?"

"Yes, John. I'm sorry. Tim told me himself."

"Maybe it was just an excuse. Or a passing thing?"

Hearing the pain in the voice of this quiet man made my heart ache. Knowing how reserved he was, it must have taken him all month to drum up the courage to call.

"I really can't say," I sighed. "Since the divorce, we haven't communicated much. You'd think he'd call his children once in a while."

"I know. I wish he'd call us, too."

"Well, in a way it makes sense. He's probably too ashamed."

"I've tried to call him," he said. "He has caller ID, and I think he avoids answering when he sees our number. I've left messages, but he never responds."

By now, John's sad voice was pulling at my guilt-machine. "Look, I'm sorry that I blurted it to Emilia the way I did. Will you please tell her that?"

"I'll try, Lauren. She's sure you said it out of spite, since you're in so much pain."

"Well, I won't deny that I'm hurting, but I shouldn't have blamed it on you two."

"We do wonder if it's our fault."

"Any parent would." I was trying to picture myself in his shoes. "To be honest, I don't know what to think about the whole homosexuality thing. I mean we're at the beginning of the Twenty-first Century, and times are changing—"

My voice ground to a halt. I couldn't think of anything else to say.

"It's all right, Lauren. Certainly, it's not your fault. Or the kids'. All we can do right now is give Tim time."

I wanted to say I'd like Tim to send some child support, but instead said, "I just wish he'd pay some attention to Danny and Ginna."

"I agree, but there's nothing we can do about that."

"Yes, I know."

Silence filled the line between us. Tears were dripping down my cheeks and off my chin.

"Just remember we still love you and your children," he murmured.

"Thanks, John. I'll pass that along to the kids."

More than three years went by after this conversation. While working at the power plant, my boss, Dave Cameron, had started to show romantic interest in me, and I was beginning to feel drawn to him, too. After all the rejection and hurt of the divorce, I was attracted to his warm personality. He was the opposite of Tim in many ways. Ginna and Danny were both teenagers, becoming more mature by the week. Tim rarely contacted us again, and neither had his parents. The need for a change, for a real relationship, began rising in me.

It took all this time for me to work through the stages of anger and grief from the dissolution of my marriage. Having a strong man in my life became more tempting by the week. There were still days I wondered if it was wrong, but the more I saw him at work, my needs to be held, cherished, and protected became harder to resist.

Somewhere in the deep recesses of my mind, I knew I was looking for consolation in the wrong places, but I chose to ignore it.

Tears began to blur my sight as I remembered the mistakes I'd made, but there was no way to change them now. Still, my mind kept mulling over these things as though I sought a way to justify myself, or at least understand why I'd been so foolish. Perhaps when a person is facing the possibility of an early death, this need for vindication arises like gas bubbles from the mire of a swamp.

CHAPTER 2
The Lie - 2007

I'd been lying to my daughter for several weeks. I sat behind my desk at work, staring at the phone, knowing I needed to call and tell Ginna I'd be late again. Dread held me back.

At sixteen years old, was she old enough to understand?

Before I could change my mind, I grabbed my cell phone and punched the speed-dial for home.

"Hello, Mom?"

I breathed a sigh of relief when Ginna answered, instead of my thirteen-year-old son. This would make it easier.

"Hi, Honey. I'm going to be late again tonight. Don't wait supper on me."

"I know, just fix something for the two of us. Oh, yeah. It's just me. Danny isn't even here. He's sleeping over at a friend's. How come I'm always the one left home alone?"

I pushed away the ache her sarcasm caused.

"So you're working late on that public relations project?"

"Partly that. Dave has asked me to join him for dinner, too."

"You mean Mr. Cameron, your boss? I thought his name was John."

"He's John David Cameron. I found out he goes by his middle name."

"Isn't he nearly ten years older than you, Mom—and married?"

Here goes. "Yes, he is. But you don't realize that ten years isn't as big a deal when you're thirty-five. It's not as much of my lifetime as for you at sixteen."

"Yeah, Mom, I can do the math."

"Please. I need to see where this will go. You have no idea what I went through when your father left."

"Danny and I went through a lot, too."

"I know you'd like to go back to the home we had before. You've told me that often enough, but it's all gone. Your father took it from us when he walked out."

My throat closed off all words in a choke. These were feelings I never wanted to dredge up—the deep, sharp pain of rejection, the feeling that I was worthless, and didn't deserve to be loved, ever again. How could he choose to love a man instead of me? This was the part I couldn't bear to tell Ginna.

"Mom, are you all right?"

So Ginna *could* hear the pain. She had always been perceptive.

"I'm fine, Honey. Don't wait up for me, okay?"

"Okay."

Well, that could have been worse, I thought, as I signed off.

Soon Dave tapped on my half-open office door. Swiping at the tears, I smiled up at him.

"Ready?" His voice had a rich, deep tone that always warmed me deep inside.

"Sure am." I grabbed my purse and walked out the door with him into the nearly empty hallways of the High Plains Nuclear Plant in eastern Colorado.

This was the job that had opened almost miraculously after the divorce. With an associate degree in public information, it was a perfect fit for me. I was thankful I'd pursued this program at the community college in Palestine. Something must have been forewarning me that I needed a Plan B—something besides relying on my husband's salary.

True, the move had been harder on my children than I'd expected. We had ended up in a small rental house at the edge of tiny Deer Path, Colorado. Definitely a comedown from the house we'd had in Texas.

There were days when I felt guilty that the lives of my children weren't enough to keep me happy and occupied. But I needed this job as a way to feel valuable, contributing something to the world. Besides, we also needed my paychecks to get by, and I wanted adult companionship. Sure, I was probably looking for this in the wrong place, but at that point in my life, I was grasping at any promising-looking straw.

By now, Dave and I were standing in front of the elevator that would descend from our third-floor offices to the ground level. While we were waiting, my phone buzzed.

"You have a call?" he asked.

Glancing quickly at the phone's screen, I shrugged. "Just a text. Probably from my daughter. I'll read it later." I knew I should read it now, but my heart was pounding with him standing so close. I didn't want to mess up this moment.

With a chime, the elevator arrived and the door slid open. It was empty, and my heart race faster as we stepped inside. As soon as the door shut, he took my hand and drew me closer. When the light for the second floor flashed on and back off, he tilted my face up, his fingers weaving into my blonde hair, kissing deeply.

"Oh, Lauren, I know you're probably hungry, but I just want to be alone with you. That's what I'm hungry for."

I gazed up into his shining gray eyes. He wasn't a truly handsome man, but he had a magnetism which set my head spinning. It was so good to have value to someone again, especially to someone important in the company like Dave.

CHAPTER 3

The Morning After

I woke with a start, wondering where I was. Then I heard the deep breathing beside me and glanced over at the lanky form sleeping there. His arm was lying under my back. White sheets were wadded all around us, and I realized I was naked.

Then a rippling shock flowed through me, *What have I done? Now there's no turning back.*

Here I was in the silence of a hotel room, a parade of emotions marching through my mind. First came fear, followed by regret: *Have I compromised all I thought I believed? But Dave really cares for me—I hope.*

As I rolled and turned my face toward his, a slight smile played at the corners of his mouth, sending a throbbing thrill through me and echoing the warmth and pleasure of his intimate embrace. For the first time in many years I felt loved and safe.

Now his eyelids fluttered open, and his smile grew larger and warmer. "Awake now?" he murmured. "Are you alright?"

I nodded and drew closer to him. "I'm fine, for the first time in ages."

"I'm glad," he smiled, and then kissed my lips gently.

I flowed into him, our bodies no longer two separate entities.

I didn't want to fall asleep again, knowing Ginna was home alone. Sure, she was old enough to take care of herself, but guilt kept bubbling up in my mind. Soon after that second lovemaking, I turned and sat on the edge of the bed.

"I have to get home, Dave."

"Why? No one is going to see us here."

"I think my daughter already suspects something."

"Is that why you're afraid to read her text?"

I was surprised he'd noticed this. "No," I snapped. "But I need to go now. I can't leave her alone all night."

He sighed and rolled toward me. "Hey, don't be such a worrier." His hands were trying to move between my legs.

I rose and reached for my clothes. "Look, it's not as though I don't want to stay. But—"

"Okay, Lauren. I'm sorry I'm being a jerk about this. I'll take you home."

"Well, first you'll have to take me to the power plant to get my car. I can't have you driving to my house, at least not yet."

He was standing beside me by then, and gently pulled me into his arms. "I understand. I'll try to be more of a gentleman about this. You are very special to me, you know."

I hope he really means that, I thought. *I should be more careful, but he's irresistible. And I've been so lonely these years since we moved here. But there's no going back to Texas for me, and now it seems there's no going back in my feelings for this man.*

***

We couldn't be together every night, even though I ached for it. He needed to find ways to keep his wife from getting suspicious, so I had to be ready to change plans at a moment's notice. At first, this didn't bother me. After all, it wasn't as though I had much of a social life, just transporting my kids to and from their activities. Ginna had her driver's license now, but we couldn't afford a second car, so I was still their chauffer.

Soon, I was willing to drop anything to be with Dave, at whatever secret rendezvous he found. My needs began to outweigh thoughts of my children, dear as they were to me. I'd never realized hormones could do such powerful things to my body. Some days I'd chastise myself for reacting this way. I shouldn't feel this intense attraction to someone else's husband. But my body seemed unable to listen.

One Friday after work, he drove much farther than usual, west toward Denver.

"Where are we going?"

"Someplace special," he grinned.

It was late fall and the days were growing shorter, so everything was dark, with stars appearing by the time he pulled into a lane by a sign reading *Palisade Estates*. The road was unpaved and rough, so he took it slowly. Evergreen trees loomed high overhead, blocking my view of the sky. Then just as he rounded a corner, a mountain vista opened with a small log cabin in the foreground.

"Well, what do you think?"

"Oh, Dave, it's really romantic out here in the wilderness with only the stars to see by."

"I'm glad you like it. It's been one of my favorite places for a long time." He gathered me into his long arms.

For an instant, I wondered if he and his wife had come here often but dared not ask. Instead, I took a deep breath to clear my mind as we got out of his car.

"Why didn't you tell me we were coming so far?" I asked, an edge in my voice.

"I'm sorry. Is there a problem?"

"Well–I guess not. My kids are both sleeping over at friends' houses, since it's Friday. But I really should let them know where I am. I've never left them alone all night like this."

He covered my hand with his large warm one. "Your hands are cold," he whispered. "I'm sorry I didn't forewarn you. I guess I'm only thinking of my needs."

My kids are old enough to manage. I wanted to believe this mental voice—to stop the feeling of guilt growing in my chest. Then my physical need for him overrode all thought.

By this time, he'd pulled me closer and was gently moving his thumb across my cheek. "You are so wonderful for me," he murmured.

Even though I wanted to reply, my voice caught somewhere in my throat. Gazing over his shoulder, I could see the full moon rising behind him. Soon his hair was outlined in a halo of moonlight.

As we stood on the small cabin's porch, his hands moved to my shoulders before I realized he'd even lifted them. In the next instant, my sweater was being pulled over my head and his hands were working their way into my blouse. The air was cold, but his hands were so warm. One of his arms was behind my shoulders, pulling me toward him in a fierce embrace. I'd never felt such urgency and power in him. His lips pressed hard and hot against mine. Gradually he moved his lips down my neck, and I moaned in pleasure.

Then he carried me in his arms through the cabin's door, both of us pulling off clothing and tossing it aside as we made our way to the tiny room's bed.

CHAPTER 4
The Tables Turn - 2008

The day of Ginna's seventeenth birthday, she and Danny were tossing a baseball back and forth in our backyard. I'd wanted to throw a party for her like last year's, her Sweet Sixteen Birthday. But Ginna said she didn't want one.

"Mom, it's too much expense for you." Where was this new thriftiness coming from? "Besides, I don't have any friends here that I want to invite."

Yes, last year's party had been awkward. By this time, I was hoping she and her brother would have begun to fit in with their peers at school.

Watching them play, I reflected on how Danny was doing. He'd always been more of a loner than his sister, quiet like his Grandpa John. In the deeper recesses of my mind I sometimes wondered if he was keeping the same kind of secrets his father had about his sexuality. Almost every day, I prayed this wasn't true.

Today was just another example of how my children took refuge in each other. For a while after Ginna started high school, they'd started acting distant and argued a lot. They must have patched things up through the next couple of years because now they were closer than ever.

So many things I wished I could change, but all I could do was try my best. *That's what being a single mom is*, I told myself for the millionth time.

Just as I turned away from the kitchen window to do some dishes, Danny threw the ball over Ginna's head. She scrambled back to retrieve it, and when she bent over to pick it up, her hand went to her back, rubbing it. With a start, it came to me that this gesture was all too familiar. I'd done it often when I was pregnant.

No, that can't be, I told myself. *She's never been that kind of girl. I don't think she's even dated any of the boys in her school.*

In spite of myself, though, I began noticing other clues over the next few weeks.

At last, I couldn't stand it any longer. One night after Danny had gone to bed, I took her into the kitchen, where he'd be less likely to hear us. Once we were seated in the straight-backed chairs at our small wooden table, I stared at her, searching for words.

Trying to keep the anger out of my voice, I began, "Ginna, is there something you need to tell me? I'm a mother, and I know what pregnancy looks and feels like. There's no denying that none of your jeans are fitting now."

"Hey, who are you to criticize me?" she retorted. "You've been sleeping with your boss for months."

That's a low blow.

"So this gives you permission to sleep around?"

I was surprised when she shook her head. "I don't know."

"What don't you know? Who's the father of this baby?" My voice grew sharp, as unstoppable waves of anger and disappointment swept over me. "How many men have you slept with?"

Ginna stared at the tabletop, tears filling her eyes. "Mom, in the sense you're saying, I've never slept with anyone."

"What is that supposed to mean, young lady?" Tears began pooling in my eyes, too. Ginna turned, looking out the yellow-curtained window above the kitchen sink.

"Are you telling me someone raped you?" I whispered.

Ginna turned back to face me and shrugged. "Would it make you feel better if it was, Mom?"

This comment sent a jolt through my gut. Suddenly, I remembered how Ginna had tried to warn me against having an affair with Dave, with the text I'd received in front of the elevator. A text I should have read then, but shoved aside. Guilt and regret bubbled up from deep inside me. The tables were turning on me.

"But who? When? Was it date rape?"

"You have no reason to hassle me," cried Ginna. "You're the one who's been sleeping with a married man."

Again, her words hit like a physical blow. I was reaping what I'd sowed.

By this time Ginna had stalked into the living room and collapsed on the worn brown couch, burying her sobs in a yellow pillow.

"Cry if it helps." I sat beside her, smoothing her short, brown hair with my hand. "We can sort this out. I'm sorry I got angry. This is just so unexpected."

She nodded slightly under my touch. "That's for sure. I can't explain it, Mom," she murmured into the pillow. "It's complicated."

"What's so complicated? Either you practice safe sex or you don't."

"I never meant to lose my virginity."

"What? You must have let yourself be drawn into a situation where it could happen."

"Not really, Mom. Like I said, it's really confusing. You wouldn't believe me if I told the truth, anyway."

"Try me."

"It's like a bad dream. Maybe I'll wake up and it will all dissolve into nothing." She gulped a breath. "Danny and I have met some time-travelers from another dimension."

"Wait, this sounds like a great fable." I almost laughed. "Can't you come up with a better excuse?"

"Mom, I'm not lying. I knew you wouldn't believe me if I told the truth."

"Well, I have to admit it's the most imaginative excuse I've ever heard. Whose science fiction book did you get this from?"

"Forget it then." Ginna pulled the pillow on top of her head, and sobbed into the couch.

She kept her face toward the back of the couch and didn't speak for another moment or two. When she began, she didn't raise her head, but kept it against the cushion. Her words were muffled, so I could barely hear them.

"These time-travelers—"

"Wait, you're saying some time-traveler raped you?" *Is this just an elaborate scheme to make me feel guilty, after all?*

"Mom, I'm so confused. I didn't even understand what was happening to me at first. I was afraid I was gaining too much weight. I know I'm just a huge disappointment to you now."

At this, Ginna sat up and pulled me into a desperate hug.

"Except that I'm the one who failed, not you," I murmured. "How could you have a good example, when I—"

"Don't say any more, Mom. I can tell you still don't believe me."

I can't deny that. For whatever reason, Ginna can't face the truth.

Through the rest of the pregnancy, all I could do was mull these thoughts over. This tale of hers was unbelievable, but she never tried to give any other explanation. I decided it must have been date rape, and Ginna couldn't handle the memory. This was just some tale she'd read somewhere and latched onto in her panic to overcome the trauma.

Perhaps it was someone at school, because as the pregnancy began to show more, I had to force her to start her senior year of high school. She came home in tears almost every day. Her emotions were on edge because of the pregnancy hormones, but I wondered if there was more to it. We both were thankful when the high school teachers finally agreed to continue her studies at home during late September and October, as her pregnancy entered its last months.

***

Despite my fears for my daughter's sanity, we did draw closer. I supported Ginna in her decision to keep the baby, even though it meant taking on the responsibility of child-rearing all over again.

Still, there were days when my life felt like a waking-nightmare. My first impulse was to seek comfort with Dave. Even as nagging guilt hung over me, my sheer need for him kept overwhelming any doubts.

Of course, he could sense something was off and asked one evening when we'd slipped off to our favorite motel in Greeley, "What's bothering you? Have I done something wrong?" We were already lying in the tangled bedsheets.

"Not you, just me." I tried not to echo the testiness in his voice.

His dreamy eyes stared into mine, full of puzzlement. "What's that supposed to mean? Sounds like an excuse I've heard before."

This wasn't what I needed to hear. "So you've had other affairs."

"Hey, they were just fun and games, Lauren."

"I'm not a fun and games person."

He took both my hands in his. "You're a deep person," he whispered into my ear. "I've never known anyone like you."

"You probably say that to all your lovers." Though I was trying desperately to brace myself against his charms, I wasn't succeeding. "Your hands are so warm," I sighed. "I sure could use you in my drafty old house."

"Is that the problem? You want more of me?"

"Yeah, that's part of it. I don't feel right being just your mistress." He blinked but didn't give a quick reply, so I went on, "The bigger problem is my daughter has gotten herself pregnant."

"What's that got to do with us?"

I cringed. His response was too quick and sharp. Again, I needed to take some deep breaths before I could speak. "I tried to raise her with morals, Dave. Now that she sees what I'm doing with you, well—I've totally blown my credibility."

"Credibility? Hey, this isn't the Nineteenth Century, you know. Values have changed."

"I know, but she's my only daughter."

"Take it easy," he murmured, pulling me closer. "I know you love me, and you know I love you. That's enough for us. Just put it aside and enjoy what we have. Your daughter's problems are her own. You're not responsible for every decision she makes."

Despite my misgivings, I leaned into his embrace and nodded against his chest. "I want to believe that. Still, there's something inside me like a judge saying 'Guilty!'"

He made no reply, but turned my face up toward his and kissed my lips, then nuzzled just below my jaw line. He already knew this was one of my erotic zones. There was no way to resist him. My body was responding in spite of my doubts.

Later, as we both lay on the hotel's bed, I could hear his deep, even breathing in sleep. All I could do was stare at the ceiling and blink back tears. Why was I so weak?

CHAPTER 5

First Attempt - 2008

After that encounter, I knew I was incapable of telling Dave to his face that we should break things off. Shame filled me as I realized I had no will-power to resist his physical charms. He had some attraction women couldn't resist, making sex beautiful, much more than merely the physical. Or maybe he was so charming and alluring, I was fooled into thinking he really cared about all of me.

Too often, though, my thoughts drifted to his wife, wondering if she knew what he was like. Perhaps they had a concept of 'open marriage'. One thing for sure, he'd made it clear he had no intention of leaving his wife, whatever her name was.

That last thought brought a sinking feeling in my stomach. I knew nothing at all about this woman, and didn't want to. Gritting my teeth, I told myself to grow up and do the right thing.

Voice mail or e-mail was too impersonal, so I tried to find a nice card to write my message on. Of course, all the cards in the store were much too romantic or talking about enduring friendship.

I sighed as I looked at one after another. Someone needed to invent an *"I'm breaking off this relationship"* card. There had to be lots of people out there who needed one at some point. I laughed at this thought.

At last, I settled for a card which was blank inside with a few simple flowers on the front.

The hardest part came later that evening, sitting at the kitchen table trying to think of how to express my true feelings in words. After the first attempt resulted in a ripped-up card, I realized I shouldn't be writing it directly on the card and grabbed a blank sheet of paper. Good thing I'd bought a whole packet of cards.

When Ginna came in to say good-night, waddling now in her late pregnancy, there were piles of crumpled paper on the floor.

"Whatever are you up to, Mom? Trying to write a book?"

Smiling up at her, I felt a rush of warmth. Instead of replying I stood and gave her a big hug. "I love you, Honey."

Ginna seemed surprised, but then returned the hug. "Love you, too, Mom. G'night."

As my daughter left the kitchen and turned down the hall toward her bedroom, tears coursed down my cheeks. *I have to do this for her sake. I can't go on living a lie.* I sat down again and began writing on yet another blank sheet of paper.

None of my attempts made it off the floor that night.

***

The next morning after Danny went to school, I had a crashing headache and called in sick. I was lying on the couch with a heated rice-bag over my eyes when Ginna came out of her bedroom.

"Mom, what's wrong?"

"Oh, just an aching head. I couldn't face work today. The pain pills I took haven't started working yet."

"Can I get you anything?"

"Yeah, maybe a Coke. Sometimes that helps the ibuprofen work better."

Ginna poured herself a cup of coffee with cream and brought me the can of soda. She sat in the wooden rocking chair across from me, as I propped myself up on the couch. Sun was streaming in the window, highlighting dust motes in the air. I shaded my eyes from the glare and shifted so my back was to the light.

"You shouldn't have too much caffeine while you're pregnant, Ginna."

"I know. This is half decaf."

I didn't add more, not wanting to be a nag. We sat for a long time, silently sipping our chosen drinks. My head began to throb a bit less. She was looking at me with concern in her eyes, and at last I had to speak. I wasn't sure why, but something was pressing at my heart, almost a tangible ache. Should I open up my darkest secret about her father? Perhaps then, she would be more ready to confide in me. But I still hesitated.

"Ginna, I know you don't want to talk about this pregnancy and how it happened, and I'm willing to accept that for now. But if there's something bad that happened to you—like rape—you know I want to help you. Please remember that I love you."

"I know, Mom." She looked down at the floor. "Maybe someday. But I'm okay, really."

***

That evening, Danny stayed at school late for soccer practice and Ginna was helping me make dinner. My head ache was threatening to return. *Maybe if I share my deepest hurts, I'll feel better*, I thought. Taking a deep breath, I turned toward my daughter.

"There's something I have to tell you. I can't keep on bearing it alone." A stricken look came into her eyes. "No, it's not about you—well not quite."

Ginna looked up, her eyes clouded with confusion.

"You know your father left me for a lover."

"Yeah," she nodded. "That's not news."

"What you don't know is that lover was a man."

Ginna almost dropped the dish she was holding. "What?"

"Yes, a man. Tim told me he realized he was gay. He said he always had been."

"But you two were married. You had Danny and me. How could he change like that?"

"I have no idea. It took me completely by surprise. I never saw it coming."

By this time both of us were crying.

"I'm not sure if knowing makes me feel any better—or worse," I muttered.

"I've heard people say they've been born gay," Ginna said. "Maybe their hormones are different from ours."

"Does that really make it normal? I mean, some people have brain chemical imbalances that make them obsessive or paranoid. Does that mean they're 'normal', too?"

Ginna's gaze turned away, and she stared at the floor for a long time. My headache was still rising, so I closed my eyes. Then I felt a tight hug.

"I can see how much you're hurting, Mom."

"Of course, it hurts. It's turned my whole world upside down. I've had to re-examine everything I thought I believed.

That's probably why I've gotten myself into an affair. It's like I have no foundation anymore."

"Yeah, I kind of feel that way, too. Here I am an unwed mother. People at school must think I'm just a slut. But it really isn't like that. It was all an accident—"

"Ginna—"

"No, not right now. Maybe later I can talk about it."

"Okay. After all, I've just dropped a bombshell on you. I know you and your dad were close before."

"I guess this is why he's cut himself off from us?"

"Maybe he's too ashamed to tell you the truth."

"Sounds like he couldn't handle it," Ginna sighed. "Maybe it was worse in Texas than here in Colorado."

"Could be. People there are more conservative in their views."

"And their religion, Mom."

At this comment I swallowed a lump in my throat. *Maybe we need to find a church here. I shouldn't keep avoiding this. But the thought of walking in there a single mother with my pregnant teenager is more than I can handle right now.*

Besides, I was ashamed that I hadn't thought of going to church in ages.

"How did you keep this all to yourself for so long, Mom? It's been years."

I shook my head. "I didn't want you to go through the extra confusion and pain. The divorce was hurtful enough."

"But you shouldn't have to bear things like this all alone."

"I guess that's why I had to tell you now." I wanted to say more, but held back. Hopefully Ginna would reach a point when she could face her own truth and stop hiding behind her wild tale of time-travelers.

"Please don't tell Danny about Dad. I want to wait until he's older, if I ever tell him at all."

"Okay, I'll respect your wish, but I think you should tell him." Ginna moved to the couch and gave me another hug. "I love you, Mom. But where do we go from here?"

"I don't know. Nothing we do or say can change anything."

"If God is so good, why did he let all this stuff happen?"

Again I was at a loss for words. "I remember a Bible verse that says, 'In this world you will have troubles.' We're only human, and there are tons of things we don't understand. Maybe someday all this will make more sense."

"I remember that verse, Mom. In it Jesus goes on to say, 'But take heart. I have overcome the world.' We should pray about it, shouldn't we?"

Oh, Lord, I think I've forgotten how to pray. I was too ashamed to say this to my daughter, though. "Thanks for reminding me of the rest of that verse, Honey. I've been forgetting things like that for too long."

By then we were putting dinner in the oven. "Say, we have an hour before this is ready, and Danny won't be home for at least that long. Why don't we take a walk?"

"That does sound like a good idea, Mom. I'll get the jackets."

The warm sun on my back seeped into me and lifted my spirit.

"Ginna, there's something else I need to tell you about your dad."

She turned her gaze on me, but didn't speak.

"I haven't been completely fair with your memories of him. He does love you and our brother very much, but he's been too ashamed to face you because of his sexuality."

"But, Mom, we'd understand, I think."

"Let me tell you about a letter I got from him about two years ago."

"What about it? Why didn't you tell us sooner?"

The sharp tone in her voice made clear I'd been wrong to withhold this from her.

"I suppose I was ashamed and confused by everything back then. And I was afraid of how Danny would react, being a boy, you know."

I heard her give a deep sigh. "Go on, then."

"In this letter your dad told me he always knew he was gay, and that he'd married me in an attempt to change himself. But he said it didn't work. That made me feel like I'd failed him in some way."

"You couldn't have failed him, Mom. You didn't know who he really was."

"Yeah, I guess so. It's taken me a long time to get myself adjusted to this new reality. But that's not the main point. What Tim asked me to tell you is that he still loves you and Danny, but he doesn't want you two to deal with the stigma of having a gay father. You know I've told you that he rarely sent any child support money, but he did send some. He asked me to do my best to save it up for your futures—both yours and Danny's. I tried to honor that, and put it into a separate savings account."

"And you never told us this?"

"I feel now is the time to tell you, Ginna. Now that you're going to be a mother, you will have a lot on your shoulders. Right now the economy is shaky, interest rates are plunging, and the bottom is falling out of the housing market."

She stopped and grabbed my arm. "What's going to happen to us, Mom? Now you've got me worried."

"No, this isn't bad. Hear me out. With what your father has sent, I have saved enough to make a down payment on a house."

"You mean we get to move? Are we going back to Texas?" Her voice became hopeful.

"I wish, but no. I'm sorry. Our landlord here wants to sell the house we've been renting. I've always hoped we could move to a better place, but I have to stay near my job at the power plant. The money from Tim is just enough for a down payment on the house we're in. The monthly payments won't be any more than we're paying for rent."

"Oh." Now she sounded down.

"At least this way, we will be paying into something that we can keep, instead of just sending the money into someone else's pocket."

Ginna turned away for a moment and brushed at her eyes. When she faced me again, she tried to smile. "I guess it's better this way."

I took her hands in mine and squeezed them. "It's the best I can do, Honey. And it's your dad who made it possible. Whatever you think of him for all the disappointment and pain he's caused, remember that he did this one thing to help us."

She nodded, but didn't speak.

As the afternoon sun sank toward the western horizon, the autumn air became crisp with a chill breeze. We'd walked about a mile down the country road that led from our little house past harvested farm fields—now just gray stubble. We turned and headed home, arriving just before Danny's soccer coach dropped him off.

After dinner, Ginna went into her room and did some of her school assignments on her computer. I kept hoping she would open up and talk more about her pregnancy, but apparently she wasn't ready.

***

The next day I went back to work and stayed in my small office past noon, finding things to do on my computer. There were lots of articles on nuclear protests in my in-box that I'd been ignoring. Today would be a good day to read them.

Most of my PR job here had been trying to promote the new safety of nuclear power plants. Things finally had quieted down from the Chernobyl accident in 1986. Fewer people each year mentioned America's Three-Mile Island incident back in 1979.

Still, the vehemence of the anti-nuclear articles surprised me. Despite the improving record of nuclear power worldwide, the opposition appeared to be growing rather than diminishing. I tried to overlook the diatribes and search for writings that presented scientific evidence, gradually finding some.

When my head began spinning from being crammed with facts, I had to take a break. Heading down the hall from my office, I turned left into the break room to refill my coffee cup. There beside the coffee maker stood Dave. Since lunch hour was over, no one else was around.

"Oh, hi," I managed to blurt out.

"What have you been up to? I haven't seen you all day."

"Just reading up on the competition."

"Ah."

"Yeah, I had to take a break. My head was about to explode."

"It does get to be a bit much," he nodded. "Come take a load off."

Before I could reply, he took my arm and guided me to a chair at the lunch table. He seated himself directly across from me and gazed into my eyes. Already, I felt my determination melting away.

Fortunately, we were in a public area, where I knew he wouldn't be overt in his advances. Even so, it was still uncomfortable looking into those sexy gray-blue eyes. I took several sips of coffee before I spoke.

"There's some good points to a few of the articles, especially when they address the problem of how to deal with nuclear waste."

He nodded and smiled. "We're still working on that for sure."

"Part of me likes the idea of renewable energy sources, but they're not trouble free. I've also run across articles talking about the problems hydroelectric dams cause for native fish populations. Even some saying that wind turbines kill too many migrating birds."

"Then others claim humans are more important than fish and birds," he chuckled.

I sighed and took two more sips of coffee. "I guess there's solar power."

"That's coming along. You see road signs on the highway powered by solar panels now. More people are putting solar panels on their roofs."

"It's still too expensive to be competitive, though."

"Eventually, fossil fuel supplies will get expensive, too. Then we'll see."

"I suppose so. There aren't any easy answers, are there?" Another knot formed in my stomach. What did the future hold for my children, or my grandchildren? Having a grandbaby on the way was changing my thinking about environmental issues. I didn't want this child to grow up in a polluted world. Whenever my mind took these negative turns, I knew I should remind myself to trust that God was in control. It was getting harder to do this as more doubts and fears rose in me each day.

With a start, I felt Dave's thumb brushing away a tear on my cheek. "What's that for?" he whispered.

I hadn't even realized I was crying. Pulling away from his touch, I wiped my face hastily. Once I'd blown my nose, I tried to laugh it off. "I think I've caught some of my daughter's emotional hormones."

"I'm sure it's hard. Has she ever opened up about the father?"

Mutely, I shook my head, knowing I couldn't trust myself to speak right then.

"Once you told me you thought it was date-rape."

This time I nodded and finally found my voice. "All she's told me is some crazy story about being taken by time-travelers. I'm wondering if the rape unhinged her so much she's temporarily lost her sense of reality."

"People do come up with strange ways of coping with trauma."

"I'm so worried about her, Dave. I just hope that once the baby's born, her mind will clear."

"Well, her mind will definitely be occupied, with a newborn to care for."

"I hope when she first sees that little baby she'll fall in love with it, and her maternal instincts will take over. That's what happened to me when she was born."

"So Ginna is your first child?"

I realized that I'd never told him about my family. "Yes,

and I have a son who's three years younger. Do you have children?"

His eyes showed the same surprise I'd just felt. "Yeah. I guess I haven't told you about them either."

"If it's too personal, we don't have to go there."

"No, it's okay. I also have a daughter and a son. My son is fifteen years old, and my daughter is about to graduate from college in Boulder."

"University of Colorado?"

"Yep."

"What's her major?"

"Landscape architecture," he grinned. "Maybe she'll be one of the people designing the landscapes of mining area cleanups. Or perhaps helping design nicer-looking timber cuts in the forests."

"That sounds interesting. I don't get up into the mountains as often as I'd like, but sometimes I think the ski areas need an architect to make them look better. They're almost as ugly as clear-cuts."

"Hey, wait. I like skiing," he laughed.

"I can't afford it."

"I should take you sometime."

"Perhaps."

My coffee cup was empty, so I stood. "Guess I'd better get back to work now."

"We should go out for lunch sometime, Lauren."

"Maybe." I wasn't sure I wanted to be seen with him in a restaurant.

"I was wondering if you'd like to go to that new café on Ault's Main Street. It's several miles from here."

Was he reading my mind about not wanting people to see us together?

"Sorry, I don't have any extra cash for eating out. I brown-bag it."

"Tomorrow perhaps? My treat."

The look in his eyes was making my heart flutter. I wanted to just shake my head, but my mouth said, "Okay."

I beat a hasty retreat to my office, trying to keep my panting breath in check. How was I ever going to control my feelings for him?

The next day, he did take me out to lunch at the Rodeo Café in Ault, a small town about ten miles from the powerplant.

"It's been a long time since anything new came to this sleepy little town," he was saying as we walked down the sidewalk from where he parked. "They've done a nice job with it. I don't see many of our office staff here, though. It can be our secret," he smiled. "You probably noticed I didn't park right in front of it, either."

I relaxed at these words.

Glancing around as we stepped in, I noticed vintage photos of old-fashioned farm implements and cowboys astride their horses. The walls had been covered with reclaimed wood from old barns. Between some of the picture frames were old windows that had been attached to the wall for decoration.

"It does have a homey feel," I agreed, as we sat down at a sturdy wooden table.

A waitress soon brought menus printed like they were sheets from an old-time newspaper. "Can I get you anything to drink?"

"I'd like a Coke." Eating out was a time I allowed myself this luxury.

"I'll have the same," smiled Dave.

As we looked down the menu, I said, "Do you recommend anything?"

"Their chicken-fried steak is really good," he nodded, taking advantage of the opportunity to gaze into my eyes.

The look I saw there made a lump rise in my throat. "Sounds good to me, fattening, but good." I dropped my eyes to the menu.

"Well, this is kind of a splurge for you, isn't it?"

"I guess so. We don't get to eat out much."

"There's not much to choose from in these little towns," he chuckled.

"That's true. And we can't afford a drive to Denver or even Greeley very often."

"You know, maybe we should take a trip to Denver together." He reached across and took my hand where it was resting beside the menu.

My cheeks were beginning to burn. "Don't be too obvious," I whispered. "This is a small town where everybody knows everyone else's business."

"Okay, sorry." He pulled his hand back. "Like I said, though, few of our co-workers come here."

Just then the waitress appeared at my side, setting the Cokes on the table. *I hope she didn't hear us.* "Have you folks decided, or do you need a few more minutes?"

"We're set," I nodded quickly, glancing up to see Dave smiling.

"Yes, we'll both have the chicken-fried steak," he said. "One check, please."

As soon as the waitress was gone to the café's kitchen window to place the order, he patted my hand again. His hand felt extra warm on my chilled one.

"Why are you always so cold, Lauren?"

"I don't know. Poor circulation, maybe? Or perhaps it's because I grew up in a much warmer climate than this."

"Where was that?"

Ah, another thing I hadn't told him. "Texas," I smiled.

He reached over and curled some strands of my hair around his finger. "I love your blonde hair. Now I can call you my Yellow Rose of Texas."

I was trying not to blush again.

"No wonder you've never been skiing. I'll need to take you sometime this winter."

"I'm afraid I'll spend the whole day on my butt."

"We'll start on the bunny hill."

I could tell my cheeks were flushing even redder and looked down. The sparkle in his eyes was almost too much for me to handle.

"For now, I'd like to take you back to that cabin in the woods, if you're up for it. The aspens are gorgeous when they turn golden in the fall. This year looks like it's going to be a good one."

My gut began aching. Was it fear or anticipation? Luckily, the food arrived at that moment, saving me from thinking of a reply.

Dave was right, the chicken-fried steak was good. Cooked just right, and the gravy a good consistency, not too gooey or too runny. The mashed potatoes were not instant, either. I knew that because I served instant at home most of the time. It was quicker, and after a day at work, the last thing I wanted to do was peel potatoes.

I managed to keep up some small talk as we ate, and my stomach settled down. The food must have helped.

After we'd driven back to work, he sent a text asking what day I could come with him to the cabin. I didn't reply right away, feeling in a quandary.

I felt like I was climbing out of a deep, dark well. When I could open my eyes at last, I saw the ceiling of my hospital room overhead. In a sense, I'd been time-traveling in my mind. I wondered if it was a side effect from the anesthesia.

All those years I was so messed up, depending on someone else's husband for my needs. Not a good decision at all—no wonder Ginna was so mixed up. Tim's coming out had left me devastated, angry and confused.

But now I see it was just my excuse to let Dave lead me along.

Why did I turn my back on my faith? I should have turned to God for strength, or my Christian friends. But I was too ashamed to tell them the truth—that my husband had abandoned us for a man. Everything felt topsy-turvy, and I lost my bearings.

The one thing I did right after the revelation of Ginna's pregnancy had been to check out the little country church just up the road from Deer Path. I got the kids started going there with me once in a while.

CHAPTER 6

The Mountains Are Calling – Fall 2008

By the end of the work day the next Friday, my head was aching again. Right at five o'clock, I heard a tap on my door. I knew who it was and murmured, "Come in."

Sure enough, Dave stepped into my line of sight, closing the door behind him. "Hey, you don't look so good."

"Uh, am I supposed to say thanks to that?"

"Are you feeling sick?"

"No, just exhausted, I guess. My head is pounding."

Instead of replying, he stepped behind my desk chair and began rubbing my neck and shoulders. "Boy, you are tense," he said after a few minutes. "Your shoulder muscles are like rocks."

"Yeah. That's where I carry the weight of the world."

"I thought you were supposed to let God do that."

This remark surprised me. It was the first time I'd heard him refer to religion.

"Somehow, I never manage to let go of the stress, Dave. I have a plaque on my bedroom wall that shows a frazzled woman, and says, 'I can't relax. Tension is holding me together'."

Silently, he kept massaging, as my tension began to melt away.

Soon he was stroking my hair with one hand, and gliding the other into the neckline of the V-neck sweater dress I wore.

For an instant, I tensed. He moved the hand in my hair to my cheek, turning my head toward him. His lips found mine and massaged them gently.

"Don't tense up on me," he murmured, between kisses. "Let me help."

By now his hand had reached inside my bra and cupped my breast. In spite of myself, I sighed in pleasure.

As he rotated the desk chair around, I faced him, reaching my hands toward his waist. He dropped one hand to unfasten his belt buckle, but I placed my hand over his.

"Not here, please. I want to be in a safer place, where we don't have to worry about anyone else."

At this, he stepped back and looked down into my eyes. His were shining blue-gray, and a smile played at his lips. "So you will come with me to the cabin?"

"If that's what you want."

"Are you sure you can wait that long?" He pulled me out of the chair and leaned me against his body.

"Can you?" I asked as he set my feet back on the floor.

"I'll do whatever it takes to be with you, Lauren. It's Friday, and I know the cabin is free. Can you drop everything and come now?"

Instead of replying I drew my arms around him and nipped at his earlobe. He was so tall, that was all I could reach. "Maybe you'll need a cold shower first."

"Oh, I think I can manage." He took a deep breath and moved away, so we were no longer touching. Suddenly I felt chilled, and my inner gut ached to be touched by him again. The feeling was so intense, it took my breath away.

"How's the headache?"

"Oh, yeah. I think it's gone."

"Just call me Doctor Dave," he laughed. "Come on. Most people have gone home, and I'm not sure how much longer I can wait."

I grabbed my jacket hanging on the coat tree by the door. When I dressed this morning, going to the mountains had been the furthest thing from my mind. Luckily, it had been a nippy late fall morning, so I had a warm coat to put on.

As we went down the elevator, I was surprised he didn't steal another kiss. Perhaps he was afraid he wouldn't be able to stop with that. I wasn't sure I could have either.

When we settled in his car, I texted Ginna, but all I said was, 'Working late.' She'd figure it out.

Droplets of rain were spattering the windshield of his car as we started out of the nuclear facility's parking lot. The guard at the gate nodded, and I wondered if he was smiling. He'd probably seen us together like this before.

It doesn't matter, I told myself. *I'm not married anymore.* In the back of my mind I wondered if he'd seen Dave with other women like this. But I shoved that thought away. I was in need right now, in need of love, and Dave was all I had. Or at least that's what I thought back then.

The rain gradually changed to snow as we drove through the suburbs of Denver. By the time we'd passed the foothills, the road was showing white.

"Is it slick?" I asked.

"You mean the road?"

"Of course." I tried not to laugh.

"No, it's okay. I've got good all-weather tires."

He took one hand off the wheel and reached over to take mine. The warmth of his touch swept up my arm, through my chest, and lodged in my belly. Was he aching for me as much as I was for him? Or was this another of his fun-and-games affairs? The sensations inside me were growing so strong, this question was drowned in an instant.

He kept hold of my hand as we continued up the canyon, even though the road began to wind through trees, and snow filled the air. At each straight section, he rubbed his thumb across my knuckles. I marveled that such a simple gesture could feel so sexy.

"How are you doing?" he murmured. "Is the snowy road making you nervous?"

"Can you tell?"

"Well, your hand feels a bit clammy."

"I admit I'm not used to this weather, being from Texas and all. But it's partly that you're really turning me on."

"Ah, I was hoping so. We're almost there."

The drive had gone faster than I expected. Since he'd brought me here before, the route was becoming more familiar. When he pulled the car into the drive, it left tire tracks two inches deep in the snow. No stars were shining, just the snowflakes in the headlight beams.

"Looks like we may get a few inches if this keeps up."

"Will we get snowbound?"

"Only if you want to be."

By this time, he was helping me out of the car. He closed the door, clicked his key fob, and the car's lights went off.

Holding my hand tightly, he pulled me toward the cabin. He already had the key out of his pocket and pushed the door open with his foot once the lock clicked open. We tumbled into the dark interior, and I heard him kick off his shoes. Soon his hands were pulling off my jacket and dress. For an instant, I thought it was lucky I didn't have slacks on. His hands were so insistent that they might have torn my clothing right off. The room was shrouded in darkness, but his hands were doing their work with consummate skill. Before I knew it, we were lying across the bed, both naked and throbbing with heat.

"I knew we wouldn't need a fire just yet," he nuzzled into my ear.

He started by kissing my lips and kneading my breasts. I wasn't sure if the moans I heard were his or mine.

Somewhere in a fog I finally came back to earth, to find myself lying in Dave's arms spoon-wise, with my back to his chest, and his legs wrapped around mine.

"Did I come too fast?" he murmured.

"No. I probably did."

He laughed softly. "I think we both were well-primed."

"I do have a problem with you," I said, turning to face him.

"Uh-oh. What have I done wrong?"

It was my turn to laugh. "No, the problem is…" I moved my hand up his broad chest. "… your irresistibility."

His laugh exploded loudly. "Ha! Well, come to think of it, that's the same problem I have with you." He grasped my hand and pulled me closer so we were face-to-face.

For several minutes we lay gazing into each other's eyes. Then he began stroking my thighs lightly. "Do you need another neck or shoulder massage?"

I tucked a hand behind his head. "No, but another kiss would be nice. My husband was a terrible kisser."

He drew his lips to mine. As his arms reached around me, I cuddled closer to his chest.

"Your husband's loss is my gain," he whispered. Then drawing back, he asked, "Should I start a fire in the woodstove? Are you cold?"

"I think I'll be fine right here in bed with you. Don't leave me."

He smiled and pulled the bed's comforter over us. "I have no plans to leave you, Lauren."

"Me neither," I sighed. Deep relaxation was drawing me closer to sleep. "I don't want to ever lose this feeling."

CHAPTER 7

Down in the Valley

No matter how much I wanted to stay in the mountains, morning came beckoning us back into the real world. The rising sun revealed about six inches of sparkling snow. Each evergreen in the cabin's yard looked like the flocked Christmas trees I remembered as a child. Even inside the cabin, with a newly lit fire in the woodstove, the air was crisp. As I breathed it in, I felt that catch in my nose telling me the temperature was well below freezing.

As a child growing up in Texas, I'd only seen real snow once. When I dashed into our backyard and touched it with a bare hand, I was stunned to find it wet and cold. Not at all like the cottony white of the holiday displays in the stores at Christmas.

While I stood gazing out the cabin's front window, Dave stepped up behind me, put his arms around my middle, and turned me to face him. Before I could speak, he was kissing me.

"Sorry we have to drive home in all that," he said when he released me.

"Why don't we stay?" I put my arms around his waist and leaned my head on his chest.

He began to run his fingers through my bed-tangled hair. "I could stay another night if you can," he murmured. His hand drifted down to my neck, and he ran a finger along my jawline sending a warm thrill through me.

"Not so fast," I sighed. "I just woke up."

"So? That's my best time." He turned my face up to meet his.

I was just beginning to return his full kiss when my phone chimed.

"Is that yours?" he murmured against my ear.

"Yes. I'd better check if it's my kids."

"If you must." He released me slowly, his sexy voice tempting me to ignore the phone.

Instead, I took a deep breath and clicked on the text icon, which showed a number one. As soon as I opened it, I gasped. Ginna had texted.

"What is it?" His expression changed instantly.

"We have to get going right now. My daughter says she's in labor."

"You're sure? Isn't this early? Maybe she's just being jumpy. I thought you said she's not due for four weeks."

I was pulling on my clothes even as he spoke. "I'm taking no chances. I'll drive myself down this mountain if you won't."

He grabbed his coat and shoes, not even bothering to change the sweatpants he'd donned when he got up earlier to light the stove. "Of course I'm coming. What do you think I am? I have a daughter, too."

As we dashed out into the icy morning, I realized this was only the second time he'd ever mentioned his children.

***

At first, the unplowed snow on the road meant slow going. My heart refused to stop pounding, but I bit my lower lip to keep from speaking. There was nothing I could say that would speed us up. When we reached the plowed and salted pavement, he stepped on the gas. Now I fretted that a police officer would pull us over for speeding.

The silence was wearing on me when he finally spoke. "How old is your daughter?"

"Ginna is seventeen. Yours?"

"Uhm, twenty-two I think. I'm bad with keeping track of birthdays."

"So she doesn't live at home?"

"No, she's just out of college and already has a job offer on the West Slope."

I knew this was what Coloradoans called the half of the state on the other side of the continental divide. Since he wasn't forthcoming with any other information, I began to babble, hoping to fill my mind with something besides the fear we'd get there too late for my daughter.

"Ginna and her brother are all I have since the divorce. Tim's parents got sort of possessive, so it's probably a good thing I'm here and they're in Texas. My parents died when I was still a teen."

"How long has it been since your divorce?"

"Seven years now."

"Does Ginna know who the father of her baby is?" I wasn't surprised he asked this, because he already knew Ginna was an unwed mother-to-be.

"She claims not to. And she's gotten on my case a lot about my relationship with you."

"Ah, I see." He went silent again for several miles.

The pavement transitioned from slushy to wet, and he put on more speed. At last he spoke again, "Where exactly are we going? There's no hospital in Deer Path."

"The doctor we've been seeing is in Eaton, but the nearest

hospital with a birthing center is Greeley. I guess I'd better find out if she's made it there."

I pulled my phone out of my purse and sent a text. No reply. I kicked myself for not having a birth plan set up with the kids, but Ginna's due date had seemed far enough away.

My hands were starting to shake now. Getting desperate, I called our landline. A quavering voice answered.

"Danny, is that you?"

"Yes, Mom."

"What's happening?"

"Ginna's here on the couch, and she's crying a lot. It's all wet, too. Did she pee herself?"

My poor thirteen-year-old son sounded near tears. "It's all right, Danny. It just means the baby will be coming soon. You need to call 911 right now."

"I already did."

"Good job. I'll be there as fast as I can. When did this start?"

"I don't know. Ginna told me she had pains all night when I saw her this morning."

Why have I been so selfish?

"I wish she'd called me last night. But what's done is done."

"Am I supposed to boil some water, like they say in the movies?" he asked.

"It won't hurt. And hold your sister's hand. Right now she needs someone there for her. Try not to be scared, okay?"

"Okay." His quivering voice was gone. My hand continued to shake as I put the phone away.

"Well?" Dave asked.

"She's still at home. Supposed to be an ambulance on the way, probably all the way from Greeley. Danny is the only one with her."

"That's your son?"

Why did it take a crisis for me to realize how negligent I was with my own family?

"Yes, he's only thirteen."

Dave must have heard the anxiety in my voice, for he reached over and squeezed my hand. "We'll be there in less than an hour, Lauren."

"I shouldn't have left them alone." Tears were already pouring down my cheeks. "But her due date was still almost a month off. I'd read that first labors are often long, and the babies seldom come early."

"Everyone is different, though."

Dave was driving like a Formula One racer by this time. Yet the minutes dragged by as I watched for the cutoff to Deer Path. When we reached the tiny hamlet, I directed him where to turn. He took the corner so fast the car began to skid, but he held it on the road. I closed my eyes and tried to pray.

As we zipped through the town, I said, "There's my house, the one at the very end of this last street."

The moment his car lurched into the gravel driveway, I was out the passenger door, leaving him sitting in the drivers' seat, not even bothering to ask if he wanted to come in.

When I entered the house's front room, Danny was standing pale-faced with warm damp towels in his arms.

"Mom!" He tried to hug me and ended up shoving the towels into my hands instead. "I did what you said and boiled some water."

"Good boy." I freed one hand to pat his shoulder.

Right at this point, Ginna let out a blood-curdling scream from the couch. Acting only on instinct, I moved to her side and spread the towels between her legs, not really sure what else to do.

"Oh, Mom," she sobbed. "It hurts so bad."

"It's okay, Honey. It will be over soon. Take deep breaths, and then pretend you're blowing up a balloon. Wait for an uncontrollable urge to push. I'm here now to help you."

Behind me, I heard the front door close, and wondered if it was Dave coming in. But then Ginna screamed again.

"Keep breathing," I said into her ear. "Try not to tense up. Keep blowing up a balloon." *We should have gone to Lamaze classes.*

That contraction went better than the last. I wracked my brain for what I'd learned from my own birthing experiences. When the next contraction started, Ginna gave a low guttural moan. I knelt down where I could see between her legs. *This is going much faster than I remember my labors. I hope it's not a miscarriage.*

"Ginna, try pushing now."

"How?" she gasped.

"Your body knows what to do. Just think of pushing."

The most inhuman sound came from Ginna's throat. Now I could see the top of a tiny dark head.

"Come on, you're almost there. You'll be a mother soon. Catch your breath now. Time to push again. The baby's coming."

Another moan left Ginna's lips. Then I was busy catching the little body that emerged. Turning it over, I smiled. "It's a girl, Honey."

Opening the front of Ginna's sweaty nightgown, I placed the baby on her chest, skin to skin. The tiny mouth opened, and mewling sounds came out, so I moved her closer to Ginna's breast. Soon the little one latched on.

"There," I sighed. "It was worth it, wasn't it?"

"She's so sweet," whispered Ginna. "But how did you go through this twice, Mom?"

"I did it for love, of course, just like you."

"Do you love me like this, like I'm feeling for this baby right now?"

"Of course I do." I leaned in and kissed my daughter's damp forehead.

Then Ginna's expression clouded. "I feel like I need to push again, Mom."

"Okay. Uh—that's right, the afterbirth needs to come out."

Ginna's face got redder as she pushed this time.

"Mom, what's all that blood?" Danny cried. "Is she okay?"

Looking down at the towels on the couch, I said. "It's just the afterbirth. Don't worry."

"What's that?"

"The placenta. Now I need to figure out how to cut the umbilical cord. I've never seen this part."

Just then, a siren filled our ears.

"The ambulance is here," came Dave's voice. So he had come in.

"Thank God," I murmured to myself.

Dave must have heard and sensed my exhaustion, for he stepped over and pulled me to his side. "You did a great job, Mom," he whispered, as the paramedics rushed into the room.

CHAPTER 8
A Rose by Any Other Name

Danny and I followed the ambulance with Dave. My car was still at work, where I'd left it when we went to the cabin last night. As we drove, I distanced myself from Dave in the front seat, feeling uncomfortable with my son looking over our shoulders. Dave seemed to understand and avoided reaching for my hand.

By the time we arrived in Greeley, it was mid-afternoon. When the car was parked in the visitor section of the hospital parking lot, Dave glanced at me with a question in his eyes. I hesitated to invite him in, not knowing how Ginna would react.

"It's getting late," I said, as calmly as I could. "Your family is probably wondering what's become of you. Thanks for all your help, though."

"What about your car? How will you two get home?"

"Uh—yeah, I hadn't thought of that." I glanced sidewise at Danny, wondering what he was thinking of this conversation, but his face gave me no clues.

"I have an idea," Dave said. "My son and I can go out to the power plant and bring your car here. I can drive yours while he drives mine. He has his beginner driver's license now." I noticed he volunteered no further information about his son, not even a name. Our tacit agreement to avoid family matters was apparently still in effect.

"Thanks, Dave."

"By the way, I'll need your car keys," he said with a grin.

"Oh, duh! I guess my brain is scrambled from all this." My cheeks were getting hot. I pulled the key-fob out of my purse and handed it to him.

"I'll leave it under the floormat," he smiled. "You go enjoy that new grandchild."

As Danny and I walked away from his car, I didn't even notice Dave leave, because I was in shock at the idea of being a grandparent so soon in my life.

When we reached the hospital doors, I stood dumbly for a few moments until Danny said, "Are we going in or not, Mom?"

"Of course." I tried to smile as I took his hand. "You do realize that you're an uncle now, right?"

"Oh, wow. That's really weird."

After a short wait, we were ushered into Ginna's room, where she sat propped up with pillows, nursing the baby. She smiled as we entered.

"Looks like she's a good nurser," I said. "Better than you were."

"Oh, sorry about that, Mom."

It was the first time in weeks I'd heard even a bit of a laugh from her.

"Come on over, Danny," she added, noticing him holding back. "We won't bite."

He stepped to the side of the bed, as Ginna reached out, took his hand, and placed it on the baby's head. "This is your Uncle Danny," she murmured to the tiny, puckered face. "He'll help me take care of you."

"I will, too." I stepped to the other side of the bed.

"Thanks, Mom," she smiled. "Thanks for everything."

"I'm afraid I haven't been a very good mother recently. I'll try to do better."

Neither of my children replied. Both were too enrapt with the little bundle in Ginna's arms.

"I wonder who she looks like," Danny whispered.

Ginna shook her head at Danny as she said, "I want to name her Annemarie."

"That's a pretty name," I said. "Your father had an aunt named Mary Anna. I met her at our wedding, but we probably only saw her once or twice when you were little."

"I don't remember her," said Ginna. "Annemarie is the name of the only girl at school who was nice to me these past few months."

"Well, then it's a perfect name–Annemarie Parker."

Ginna cast her eyes down at the last name, but I couldn't tell why. Instead of meeting my gaze, she busied herself moving the baby to her other breast.

***

As I'd hoped, having the baby did help Ginna focus more on reality. She didn't mention time-travelers again. The mystery began to fade for me, though there were days when I wondered who Annemarie's father really was. Could it be a boy from school? A stranger who passed through? I was afraid to ask Ginna again about date-rape, for she seemed too fragile.

The sleepless nights took their toll on all of us. I wished there was more I could do to help, but Ginna insisted on continuing without using bottles.

"I don't want to be a quitter, Mom."

"I know. Every baby is different. You were so impatient that I had to switch to bottles after only three weeks."

"Sorry about that."

"Hey, it wasn't your fault–just the way things were."

One day when I came in from work, Ginna was gazing out the window in the living room and rocking the sleeping baby. I wasn't spending much time with Dave, still feeling guilty about what had happened on the night before the birth. It hurt to admit I'd let my children down.

"Mom?" Ginna's voice broke into my thoughts.

"Hmm?"

"Do you think we could try to call Dad and let him know he's a grandfather?"

My heart sank. I'd been dreading this question. "I don't have a number for him anymore, Honey. He's moved again and left no forwarding address or number."

"Oh." The sound of her disappointed voice brought tears to the corners of my eyes. "I just wish—well, you know what I mean, Mom."

I walked over and patted her shoulder. "Yes, I know. For some reason, he doesn't want to hear anything about us anymore."

"Yeah, you told me why," she sighed. "Why can't he at least care *some*? I mean we are still his children."

I sat down across from Ginna, taking the baby in my arms and hoping she might say more.

"I know you don't believe me, Mom, but I'm okay—really."

"If you're okay, why can't you talk about this?"

She jumped off the chair and began pacing the room.

"I'm sorry. Wait! Don't leave," I called.

"I'm not crazy, Mom! I really don't remember anything. One day I woke up and realized I was pregnant."

I saw Ginna's hands beginning to shake. Was she in some kind of post-traumatic state. "Perhaps a counselor could help you find the truth."

"I don't see how. My mind is blank. I don't remember being raped. Maybe I was, but you'd think I'd remember something like that."

Laying the baby on the couch, I rose and moved behind her, placing a hand on her shoulder as gently as I could. "I'm sorry, okay? I'll stop and just try to listen. I can see that something has really hurt you, and I'm worried for you—that's all."

Ginna turned and stared, her eyes flashing with green flecks. "Okay, Mom. Let's at least sit down again."

I moved to the couch and Ginna took a seat at the other end. Annie was still sound asleep between us, lying on her back in the little pink blanket she was wrapped in.

"Mom, please don't think I'm in some traumatic stress thing. Perhaps somehow, someday Annie and I will find out what it's all about."

We sat in silence for some tense moments. At last, I rose and took her hands in mine. "Whatever I can do to help, I'm always here for you, Ginna."

"Thanks." She held my hand against her tear-dampened cheek. After another long pause, she said, "Mom, did I dream it or was your friend Dave there when Annemarie was born?"

"Uh—yes, he was. He brought me down from the cabin—" I stopped there, unable to admit the rest of that story.

Ginna looked up into my eyes. "It's okay, Mom. I understand about the affair, now that I know the truth about Dad and all."

The look in my daughter's brown eyes spoke volumes, and brought tears down my cheeks. Words escaped me as she reached her hand up and squeezed mine hard.

Then Ginna stood carefully, lifted the sleeping baby, and carried her to the bassinette across the room. With a sweet gurgle, Annemarie nestled down as Ginna covered her with a green and yellow blanket I had crocheted for her.

"Do you think Dave would like to meet her?"

When Ginna turned to ask this, my heart did a flipflop. "What? You really want that?"

"Well, she needs someone to be a substitute grandfather, especially since she has no father."

My breath caught as I tried to sort through the conflicting feelings surging inside me. "Well, I guess I could ask him," I began. "But we're not as close as we used to be. I mean I don't like the idea. He's always kept his family to himself, and I've tried to, also."

"Okay, if you say so," she shrugged. We moved back to the old sagging couch. Once seated, she gave me a quick hug.

"What's that for?" I asked.

"Well, I guess I'm beginning to understand how it feels to be parenting alone. I'm sorry that you have to do it, too."

"Oh, Ginna." Nothing else came out of my mouth but sobs.

We sat and held each other for a long time, until the baby stirred and began to cry.

Danny must have heard, for he came downstairs from doing his homework.

"Hey, what's for dinner, anyway?" he said.

***

As the next few weeks passed, we began to settle into a semblance of routine. Danny started watching me cook and tried some on his own. It was such a relief to have his help when I came home from a long day at work. I kept feeling hesitant about involving Dave in our home life, though.

Every time I thought about approaching Dave, my stomach would tie itself into knots. He was being more distant now, too. There were days when we had some good conversations over lunch, but I avoided bringing up the subject of going to the mountains again. Whenever he offered to take me skiing, I declined, using the excuse that Ginna needed me.

Then one day, it appeared Ginna decided to take things into her own hands. On a Thursday at noon, just as we were settling at the lunch table in the break room, Dave looked over at the door in surprise.

"Well, what have we here?" he laughed.

Turning around, I saw Ginna standing in the doorway, with Annemarie in her arms. "I thought she should come see her grandma's office."

"How did you get here?" I gasped.

She shrugged. "I bummed a ride with our next door neighbor. She's waiting for me in the parking lot."

While I tried to catch my breath, Dave rose and moved toward them. "So this is the little imp who couldn't wait until her due date, huh?"

Ginna smiled up at him. "Yeah, she's a feisty one. Annemarie, say hello to Dave. He made sure your grandma didn't miss your birth."

"How old is she now?" I heard him ask.

"Almost three months." I had to say something as I clambered out of my chair.

By this time, my daughter was handing the baby to Dave. I was surprised at how gently he cradled her in his arms. As he made faces at the baby, she began to gurgle and coo. Seeing the smile on his face, I realized perhaps I'd been wrong about him after all. He seemed to be bonding with Annie already, as strange and awkward as it felt for me.

CHAPTER 9

A New Twist - Winter 2008

Seeing Dave holding my grandchild nearly stopped my heart. I wasn't sure if I was happy or dismayed. Two parts of my life that were meant to stay separated had just come together. *What am I supposed to do now? Invite him over for supper? Impossible!*

Of course, my daughter already knew about our affair, but I didn't want Danny to know. Then there was *Dave's* family. Ginna in her innocence and need for a father figure was causing a total conundrum.

I was already keeping my ex-husband's sexuality a secret from my son. Was I going to have to heap more lies on top of that?

An old saying I'd heard from my mother popped into my head: "Oh, what a tangled web we weave, when first we practice to deceive."

Here I stood in our office breakroom, trapped in the spider's sticky strands with no escape.

"So, this is Annemarie," Dave was saying to Ginna. "What a cutie she is. She's smiling at me. Are those blue eyes I see?"

"They were always blue. I've heard some babies change eye color, but she isn't so far," she said, looking from the baby to him.

"Her hair has changed color," I added. "When she was born, she had a headful of dark hair, but all that came out.

What grew back in is pale blonde." I was babbling, but my heart was still racing and I couldn't stop myself.

Just then Dave turned and handed the baby to me, smiling into my eyes. "Here you go, Grandma."

"I feel too young to be a grandparent," I stammered. "You know, Ginna was blonde as a baby, too." Somehow I needed to change the subject.

"Really, Mom? I guess I have seen a couple of old pictures of me."

A lump caught in my throat. "I think a lot of the family photos got left in the Texas house with your dad."

Ginna looked down as I spoke. "Well, I intend to take lots of pictures of Annemarie."

Was this a sharp barb at my botched motherhood?

"That's a good idea," I managed to say. "I can get you a camera for Christmas."

"I guess Christmas is almost here, isn't it?" Dave moved toward me.

Please don't touch me, not in front of my kids.

I tried to move away, hoping he could read me by telepathy. He reached over and patted the baby's head instead, and I tried not to sigh my relief too loudly.

"Ginna will be going back to school after New Year's, when the new semester starts, so she can finish her senior year." Again, I was trying to divert the subject away from Dave and myself.

"Congratulations," he said, turning to Ginna. "That's the right thing to do. How have you been keeping up these past couple of months?"

"My teachers are emailing my assignments to me," she said. "I'll have to go in next month to take my final exams in person for this semester, though."

"Well, best of luck with those," he smiled.

"I hope they'll come out okay. All I can do is my best."

"That should be enough."

"Well, we need to get back to work," I said. "At least I do. Come on, Ginna, I'll carry the baby to the parking lot for you. Thanks for stopping by. It was certainly a surprise."

"Bye," my daughter smiled at Dave. "Nice meeting you at last."

Once we were safely inside the elevator, I turned and blurted, "Please don't ever do this to me again."

"What? I thought your friend would like to meet her. He *was* there when she was born."

"You just put me in a very awkward situation. People aren't supposed to think Dave and I are anything like a family. He has a family of his own, for God's sake."

"Ah, so what you're doing with him has to be all hush-hush. You know that won't last forever. People are bound to figure it out, Mom. I did."

"Hey, I don't intend to get pregnant or anything," I retorted.

Ginna stepped back. "Ouch! That was a low blow." Her eyes were tearing up as she took the baby back into her arms.

"I'm sorry. That didn't come out right, Ginna."

"I guess not."

The elevator opened at the first floor, and she stepped out.

"No need to follow me all the way to the car, Mom. Just go back up to your *other* life."

I tried to reach for her as the door closed, but was too slow. She must have pushed the button for the third floor as she got off, for the elevator went up by itself. When the door opened again, I headed straight for the Women's Room to wipe the tears off my face.

Ten minutes later, I was still staring into the restroom mirror. My eyes were less puffy, and I'd wiped away the places where my makeup had run. If I waited long enough, Dave would be back in his office. There was no way I could face him right now.

I spent most of that afternoon staring at my computer screen and flipping through archived articles. Nothing I read sank in. My mind kept wandering. It went something like this:

What can I possibly do with this situation? Ginna needs a father figure right now, but bringing Dave into the picture just isn't going to work. And why won't she tell me who the baby's father is? Maybe she really doesn't know, but I still wonder. Then again, perhaps she knows this mystery man wouldn't be a good father. Since he's never shown up in her life through all this, he obviously doesn't care.

My hand gripped a pencil so hard that the wood suddenly snapped. As I pried a splinter out of my palm, I silently cursed myself. *I shouldn't let my sexual needs overshadow my children's need for me. As much as it hurts to admit, I know I have to confront Dave.* A pain twisted in my gut at the thought.

I wasn't surprised when he tapped on my office door at five o'clock. Before he even stepped into the room, my hands began shaking.

"That was sweet of Ginna to bring the baby over, wasn't it?" He was smiling too warmly for my comfort.

"Sure." I tried to make my voice sound calm. "Look, I can't go with you tonight."

His face showed surprise. "Well, I can't either. Not tonight. It's my son's birthday."

"Oh, thanks for telling me." I knew he would hear my sarcasm.

"What's wrong with you, Lauren?"

I turned away from him to collect my scattered wits. At last I looked up into his face. "We both know this is awkward. Our families can't know about each other."

"But it appears Ginna knows." His voice was starting to sound accusing.

"Look, she and I have been through a lot recently, in case you haven't noticed."

"I'm sorry." He stepped over and set a hand on my shoulder.

I steeled myself to ignore my body's response to his touch. "She's a sharp kid, Dave. Before I even told her, she'd figured us out. I had no choice. And then she turned around and got even with me by getting pregnant."

"Hey, I said I was sorry." Now he was reaching up to my neck, where he knew he could turn me on.

To avoid him, I rose and walked to the coat tree where my jacket was hanging. "I don't see what you're getting at," I snapped. "She's not your daughter, and you're not her father, so we'd better leave it at that."

His hands were at his sides now. "I agree." His voice sounded distant. "I was going to suggest we try that skiing lesson this weekend."

Why did my throat catch at the thought of not seeing him over the weekend? I was such a weakling! "Let me think about it. If you're still asking."

His lips formed a half-smile. "I haven't withdrawn the offer, Lauren, if you want to."

"Let's wait and talk about it tomorrow. Tonight I need to deal with my angry daughter."

"Why, what happened?"

"Oh, going down the elevator I said all the wrong things."

"It's hard with teenagers to say anything right sometimes," he grinned. "My son is like that, just turning sixteen. He's a wild colt, still in the awkward growing pains stage."

As he said this, he stepped toward me, holding out one hand. When I reached up to take it, he pulled me into one of his big bearhugs.

Despite my misgivings, I didn't pull away this time. Hugs were something I never got enough of. My parents had never been huggie, and Tim wasn't, at least not with me. Life had prepared me too well to be vulnerable to this man.

He was soon trying to kiss me, but I turned my head so all he got was a cheek. "Good night, Lauren," he murmured into my ear. "Tomorrow is Friday. So come prepared, if you want to go to the cabin again. It's not far from the Lake Eldora Ski Area. They have a good bunny hill."

"I'll think about it. I've got to get home now. I have no idea what I'm making my kids for dinner."

By the time I got home that evening, my head was whirling like a weathervane in a storm, swinging back and forth wildly. First it was rehearsing what to say when I broke up with Dave, then it switched to thinking of what the next day might be like, if we went back to the cabin.

As I entered the kitchen, I was feeling physically dizzy. Danny stood at the stove, smiling. "Look, Mom. I made mac-n-cheese for us."

My face broke into a smile. "Oh, you're wonderful, Danny. How did you know I didn't feel like cooking?"

"I just got lucky," he grinned. "Besides, I was hungry."

After we ate, Ginna rose from the table and snapped, "I have to go feed Annie now, since I'm the one with the milk." Without another word, she rushed off to her bedroom, where the baby's crib was now.

"What's up with her?" asked Danny.

"Oh, probably just the baby blues some women get—from being tired with lack of sleep." I hoped he'd accept this explanation.

While we were doing the dishes, he began talking about his day at middle school. Then his voice flared in anger, "Mom, I know what you're doing."

He was drying a plate as he said this, when he suddenly looked up at me and slammed it to the floor. Pieces flew all around the kitchen as it crashed on the dingy beige tile.

"Why on earth did you do that? It's not as though we can afford new dishes."

"Mom, I wish you'd tell us the truth. How can we think you'll believe anything we tell you, if you keep hiding things about Dave from us."

My hands were shaking. "What do you mean?" I tried to stall for time.

"I know you and Dave are more than just friends. I'm not a little kid anymore. Ginna says he's married to someone else. How can you keep on being with him?"

"It's confusing, Danny."

"Like how?" His voice was even more demanding.

"When your dad left us, I was broken. I just needed someone to love me again. And there was Dave, wanting to be with me."

"But it's not right, Mom." He turned his back on me, and I could see his shoulders shake.

"Danny, please." I put my hand on his shoulder, and he jerked away.

He started walking toward the stairs. Then, looking back over his shoulder, he snapped, "What?"

"I'm trying to make things right. If he won't marry me, then we may have to end the relationship."

"So you got divorced, and now you expect him to?"

"Danny, it's not that simple—"

Before I could finish, he fled upstairs to his attic bedroom, slamming the door. Amid tears, I knelt and picked up the pieces of broken plate. It was a piece of the stoneware Tim and I had chosen when we married. Somehow it was symbolic that it was scattered all over the floor. Just like our lives, it was in too many pieces to put back together.

CHAPTER 10
Calling Once Again
– December 2008

The next morning, I was still angry with both my kids for trying to run my life. Feeling like this, it was easy to decide I wanted time with Dave again. I'd go to work prepared, as he'd suggested. This thought made me smile.

Neither of the kids came for breakfast when I called: "Hey, get up! You'll be late for school."

Finally, I heard Danny creeping down from the attic.

"Mom, there's no school today, didn't you know? Or are you too wrapped up in your boyfriend?"

"What?"

"Yeah, Christmas vacation starts today."

"On a Friday? Don't be ridiculous."

"I don't know why," he snapped. "Something about teachers' contracts. They were owed a day off, so the superintendent added it to Christmas break. Besides, today is December 20. Christmas Eve is next Tuesday. Are we even going to get a tree?"

By this time, Ginna had strolled into the room with Annie on her shoulder. "Any ideas, Mom?" Her voice was stilted.

"Did we have a real tree last year?" I asked. "I can't remember."

"We borrowed that silly aluminum tree from the next-door neighbor," said Danny. "I hated it because we couldn't put any lights on it."

I couldn't resist a chuckle. "Those trees were really popular when I was your age. People got these rotating spotlights that changed colors, so the tree went from green to gold to red to blue."

"That's weird," Ginna said. "We want a real tree this year."

"What do you expect me to do, go cut one in the forest?"

"That's a great idea," Danny chimed in.

Oh boy, now I was in for it. "Why can't we just use the aluminum one?"

"Mom, it's not real," he moaned.

"Maybe your boyfriend can help you get a tree." Ginna's voice was full of sarcasm.

Then I decided to turn the tables on them. "Okay, I'll do just that. I'll ask Dave to help me get a real tree for you picky people. Are you satisfied?"

Ginna stood staring at me with her mouth open for a moment. Danny glanced sidewise at his sister. "Okay, then," she snapped. "Go with him. Danny and I will be fine, just in case it takes you all night to find a tree. I hope you have fun."

Before I could reply, she turned on her heel and stalked back to her room, the baby fussing in her arms. Danny sat down on one of the barstools by the kitchen counter. "Mom, I thought you said you weren't going with Dave anymore."

My guilt trip continues, I sighed to myself. "Dave asked me to go skiing with him tomorrow."

"Wish I could go skiing." Danny's voice was angry now.

"Uh—not this time. I haven't even learned how yet. I think he wants to teach me. Since the ski area is so far, we'll have to go up there tonight to be ready for the slopes in the morning, when the snow is best."

I knew I was telling a bald-faced lie, and it was too easy for me, especially when I was angry with my kids.

Some days I just want to run away from all the hassles of single parenting. Don't I deserve a break once in a while? My kids are old enough to babysit, for Pete's sake. They can manage without me for a night or two.

"Maybe next time you can come." I tried to sound convincing. "I don't know what Dave's plans are for the rest of the weekend, so it would be an imposition on him."

"He's sure nice to do all this stuff for you, isn't he?"

I looked away from his face, but his voice revealed his disapproval.

He turned and opened the fridge. "I'm hungry. Guess all we've got is cold cereal, though."

"How about I make pancakes next time I don't have to rush off to work." Maybe I could still mend fences with him.

"That sounds good," he mumbled.

Maybe my little peace offering would work.

"I've got to go to work now. Otherwise I'll be late. I'll call you when I know what time I'm getting home tomorrow." *Or the next day*, I added to myself.

"Don't break any bones learning to ski, Mom."

"Dave says we'll only be on what he calls the bunny hill."

"Be careful," he added as I moved into the front room. I sensed the hidden meaning in his words.

By this time I had my coat and the overnight bag I'd packed last night, and was headed for the door. He was pouring milk on his cereal as I walked out. Ginna was nowhere in sight, but I could hear the baby crying in her bedroom.

Good-bye, I thought. *See you when I see you.* I knew I was letting my kids get to me too much, that I should be more understanding. But the last thing I needed right then was Ginna judging me. After all, she was the one who'd gotten herself pregnant, and she had to deal with the consequences.

All that morning I kept telling myself not to worry about home. *I'm not being a bad mother. I just need a breather. They're going to be okay. The divorce was already seven years ago. I wish they were over it by now. Of course, I'm not over it. Why can't I admit that to myself?*

"No, I *am* over it," I said to the small mirror I'd hung next to the coat tree in my office.

"Over what?" came Dave's voice.

"Where did you come from?" I jumped.

"It's lunch time. Do you want to go to the Rodeo Café again?"

"Uh—sure. If you're paying. No wait, you're doing so much with the skiing and all, maybe I should pay."

He turned and closed my office door before he gathered me into his arms. "Oh, we'll find a way for you to pay me back," he whispered into my ear.

This was risky at the office, but my body clung to him, all my anger, frustration, and need washing over me like a tidal wave. I let him kiss me for several minutes, holding him tightly around the waist.

"We'd better get going if we're going to get back by one," I breathed at last.

"If you insist," he laughed, taking my coat off the tree and helping me into it.

"How can you turn yourself on and off like that?" I

couldn't help asking, for my pulse was still racing. "I'm still feeling—well—"

"Practice," he grinned.

That answer made me sorry I'd asked. I put it out of my mind as we headed toward his car, drove out of the power plant's fenced lot, and through the little town of Deer Path. As we drove along, it came to me that I had no idea where he lived. I almost asked, but held back. He'd have told me if he wanted me to know.

***

The roads weren't as snowy this time as we drove up to the cabin later that day. The last rays of sun were gleaming through the trees, making the evergreens look like lighted Christmas trees. That reminded me of this morning's conversation with my children.

"My kids want a real tree for Christmas this year," I sighed. "And I have no idea how to get one. I haven't seen any places to buy one in Deer Path."

"There might be something in Greeley. Most people have artificial trees now."

"Yeah, last year our neighbor took pity and loaned us an old aluminum tree."

"Wow, that's vintage," he laughed, reaching over and squeezing my hand.

"Have I ever told you what an infectious laugh you have?"

"What? No, I guess not. Is it that bad?"

"No, I love it." I squeezed his hand, lifting it and giving it a light kiss.

"So they weren't too thrilled with the aluminum tree, huh?"

"It didn't have a light," I nodded. "We couldn't put regular strings of lights on because the aluminum might cause a broken wire and a fire."

"Yeah, I remember those big spotlights with the color wheels."

"Me, too. Anyway, I'm not sure what to do. I mean, I don't want to disappoint my kids for Christmas. Things are pretty tight financially, like always." I moved as close to him as I could in his car's bucket seats.

"Don't you get child support?"

"Not regularly."

"What a jerk your ex must be."

"It's complicated." In spite of my efforts, a single tear dripped down my left cheek. I thought he couldn't see it, but he reached over and wiped it away.

"Sorry, Lauren. I shouldn't have said that."

"He had problems," was all I could manage to say.

Silence settled between us as the car reached the gravel road leading to the cabin. "I used to cut our Christmas tree up here," he said at last. "I bet we can find you one tomorrow. My car can carry it strapped to the roof. I have the ski racks to tie it to."

"Oh, I don't want to be a bother, Dave."

"Hey, you are not a bother. Besides, I like your kids."

"It's strange to hear you say that."

"Why?"

"Well, we shouldn't get too involved with each other's families."

"Yeah, I suppose so. But that doesn't mean I have to be a grinch. The least I can do is help you get a little tree. I mean, isn't that what Christmas spirit is about?"

I nodded as he reached over and stroked my cheek. "Now don't cry on me again. I want a happy bedmate, okay?"

"Is that all I am to you?"

"No, I didn't mean it that way. I love you."

"Yeah, but I'll always be the other woman, won't I?"

Just as I said this, we pulled up to the cabin. "You know I don't think of you that way, Lauren."

"Well, okay. I guess." For some reason, my heart was sinking.

"Come on, let's go in." He undid my seatbelt, reaching across the console between our seats.

"Boy, you have long arms." I tried to laugh, but it felt false.

"The better to hug you with, my dear."

"So, I guess this means you're my Big Bad Wolf."

"I'll settle for that." He gave me a quick kiss.

This time we didn't strip each other's clothes off as we entered the cabin. Instead, Dave opened the woodstove and started a fire.

"Come get warm with me," he said, leaving the doors open so we could watch the blazing logs. "This is what a winter evening should be, getting toasty by an open fire."

"I wish my house had a fireplace," I mumbled as I pulled a cushion off the couch and sat down beside him. "We never had one in Texas either."

"Yeah, I can see why." He wove my fingers through his, and drew me closer. "Can I share your cushion?"

I scooted over, laughing, "If you don't hog it."

"Who me?"

Soon our arms were wrapped around each other. I lay my head across his chest, listening to the steady thumping of his heart. Sitting in the fire's heat, my eyelids began to get heavy. I spoke to keep from falling asleep.

"Christmas is the hardest time of year for me, Dave."

"Since the divorce?"

I nodded but didn't trust my voice to speak again without breaking.

"My family always opens presents on Christmas Day," he murmured. "How about you?"

"We do the same. In Texas, we went to Christmas Eve services at our church. The kids put on a drama about the birth of Jesus every year."

"What about now?"

I shifted so my chilled feet were closer to the fire. "We've just started going to a little country church between Deer Path and Eaton. I'm not sure there's a Christmas Eve service because the church is only open on Sundays. They can't afford to pay the minister full-time."

"That's rural America for you," he nodded, gazing intently into the flames.

"Yeah, this town, the church, all that doesn't feel like home, even after all these years. What about you?" I looked into his eyes, wanting to know what he thought about church.

"When I was a kid, we always went to Midnight Mass."

"Oh, are you Catholic?"

"Raised that way, yes. I don't follow it too much now. When my kids were younger, we took them to Catechism and all. My wife was raised Catholic, too, so there was no conflict there. We have other issues, though." His voice trailed off.

I wanted to ask more, but hesitated, thinking it would be better to let him decide what he wanted to share.

"You've probably wondered if I'm going to divorce her."

"Well—"

"For one thing, we'd be in trouble with the Catholic Church. Right now, we're staying together for the sake of our kids. I'm not sure what will happen when our son graduates from high school."

"How can you sound so logical about all this?" I blurted this out before I realized it.

"What?"

"Oh, never mind." I turned my head away. "I guess I'll never understand men."

"It's mutual. I can't understand women. But does it really matter, as long as we love each other?"

He pulled me onto his lap and began running his hands down my thighs. I was wearing a dress again, so there wasn't much to obstruct him. It didn't take him long to turn me on, as usual, and soon we were making love right there on the floor, in front of the fire.

Later, as we lay in the cozy bed, I had trouble falling asleep. After I'd tossed and turned a few times, he pulled me toward him and asked in a sleepy voice, "What's wrong?"

"I just can't sleep. My mind won't stop worrying about stuff."

He traced the edge of my cheek with his thumb. "Can I help?"

"I don't know, to be honest."

"What do you mean?"

"Well, I just have trouble figuring out how to fit you into my life. I love coming here and all, and being with you, of course."

"Same here," he whispered, kissing my lips.

"I worry about how I'm leaving my kids while I'm with you, like I'm a bad parent. It's so hard to do that job all by myself."

Tears were trickling from the corners of my eyes again. I brushed at them angrily. He reached up a thumb to wipe one.

"Here, it's okay," he murmured, brushing my cheek. "Sometimes life is hard."

"There you go again, being irresistible."

"I guess it's what I do best."

"Do all the girls tell you that?"

"What girls?"

"All your other girlfriends."

"Lauren, please believe me. There's no one else in my life right now as special as you. I don't think I've ever met a woman like you before. You have a way about you. You speak to all of me—body and soul."

"Maybe you're just attracted to my helplessness."

"Let's not overanalyze this." He began kissing me deeply and moved his hands down my body.

"No, not now. I need to tell you something."

He rolled back slightly. "What?"

"You're the only man I've ever slept with except my husband, and he was gay."

He raised his eyebrows in surprise. "That's a line I've never heard before."

"Oh, stop it," I pushed him away. "I'm trying to be open here. This is something I haven't told anyone except Ginna. But if you're going to make a joke of it, forget it." I slid out of the covers and hunched on the edge of the bed.

He was silent and immobile behind me for a long time. Then he began to make small circles on my back with his hand. "I'm sorry. I didn't mean to be so flippant. Sometimes I'm not serious enough."

"I'm not one of your fun and games girls."

"No, you're definitely not. You're a very serious person, and I should have respected that. When did you find out your ex was gay?"

I took a deep breath. "He told me when he announced he was leaving me for a male partner."

"That must have really hurt."

"It left me feeling so—I don't know—so mixed up. I mean how could he have kept making love to me? How could we have two children? And then he suddenly decided he found me disgusting."

"Did he say that?"

"Well, no. But after he told me why he was leaving, I *felt* disgusting, like I had no worth to anyone." My breath was coming in sobs now. Somehow, he'd managed to pull me back toward him. He put his arms around me, as I lay on top of him.

I continued weeping, letting the tears flow freely onto his chest. This time, he let them be and rocked me gently.

"Lauren, I'm so sorry this happened to you. I'm glad you felt you could share it with me. I hope you realize how much *I* care about you."

I had no words left, but could only lie against him and let the aching in my heart flow out, as I cried like I hadn't in a long time.

"Not all men are like your ex," he said into my hair. "Just remember that."

All I could do was nod.

I must have fallen asleep there in his embrace. The next thing I knew, I was lying amid the warm bedclothes, my cheek still resting on his chest. I didn't move, so as not to wake him. The sun hadn't risen yet, for I realized this was December 21, the shortest day of the year.

He spent that day helping me up out of the snow several times. I could tell skiing wasn't going to be my thing. My feet felt like unwieldy blocks of wood in the tall rented ski boots. Every time I tried to turn, one of my skis always slid out from under me, and over I went.

At last, I convinced him it was time to go back to the cabin and warm up. Lake Eldora was a small ski area and didn't have a big lodge or restaurant like ones I'd seen in the movies.

After fixing us both some soup from a can, he smiled and said, "Now, about that Christmas tree."

"Oh, I think I'm too sore to go tromping through the woods looking for a tree," I moaned.

"I know where some nice little ones are. They're not far."

"Oh, okay." I managed to get myself up from the table. "After I take some ibuprofen."

He was true to his word, and we found a five-foot-tall fir tree not far from the cabin. He'd brought a small folding saw he kept at the cabin to cut it down with. "This will be the freshest tree you've ever had, I bet," he grinned.

"For sure. It's getting dark already. Should we stay tonight?"

"Well, I'll leave that up to you," he said. "Perhaps you'd like to be home with your kids tonight? It *is* almost Christmas."

"Are you sure you don't mind driving all the way down in the dark?"

"Hey, don't worry. I'm used to these mountains. I could drive this route in my sleep."

"All right, I have to ask. You once said this was a special place to you. Do you own it?"

"Yes, actually I do."

"Why didn't you tell me before?"

"I guess I didn't want you to think I was showing off or something."

"Men!" I raised my hands to my chilled cheeks and shook my head. "I'll never understand you."

"Come on, let's get this strapped on the car before we lose all our daylight."

On the way home, he drove slower because of the tree. We also had to go by the power plant to get my car, but he said he'd still follow to my house, bringing the tree.

"It will be fun to see the kids' faces," he smiled. "But I don't remember where you live exactly, so you'll have to lead."

I was past tired now, and didn't argue, knowing I had only enough energy to drive my car home.

CHAPTER 11
The Tree

My house was dark when we finally turned into the driveway, so I killed my engine quickly, got out, and walked over to Dave's car.

"Looks like the kids are already asleep. Let's just leave the tree on the front porch. I'll surprise them with it in the morning."

He looked disappointed, so I continued. "I don't want to wake the baby. Besides, I think it's better if we keep our families out of our affair."

Now his expression showed a bit of surprise, but he nodded. "I guess you're right. Things could get complicated."

"They already are. Look, I'm really tired after all the activity today. I need to go to bed."

"All right." He got out of his car and gave me a long kiss. "If you insist. Today is the twenty-first, so I won't see you next week. I'm taking my family on a ski trip to Winter Park. It's our annual Christmas thing."

"Well, at least you won't have to worry about *me* falling all over the place." I tried to make my voice sound casual.

"Our daughter will be meeting us there," he added.

"Okay. Good night." I gave him a quick peck on the cheek, and we hustled the tree to the front porch. Things were feeling strange, and I just needed to get into my own bed, alone. I was thankful not to be facing Ginna in this emotional condition as I slipped quietly in the front door.

Early the next morning, I kept my promise to Danny and made pancakes. My legs were stiff from all the skiing falls, but taking ibuprofen helped. Once the scent of breakfast filled the house, they emerged from their rooms, Annie in Ginna's arms, as usual.

"Morning, y'all," I smiled, using my best Texas drawl.

"Mmm, those smell amazing," said Danny. He didn't sound as angry as he had on Friday morning.

"There's a plate of warm ones in the toaster oven. Help yourselves."

Ginna put Annie in the wooden highchair we'd found at the thrift store in Greeley. She was old enough now to sit up and stuff a few bites of pancake into her mouth.

Knowing the next surprise I had for them kept me smiling all through the meal. Once we'd finished off the pancakes, I told them to put their dishes in the sink.

"We'll wash up later." Both of them looked at me in surprise. "First I need to show you something on the porch. It will be quick, so just set Annie in her infant seat, okay?" The baby was slumping in the high chair, so Ginna moved her to the portable car seat that she could lie back in.

Both kids were giving me a puzzled look, and I couldn't help but smile. Then I opened the front door, grabbed hold of the little tree, and pulled it into their sight. "Ta-da!"

Danny's eyes almost popped out. "Wow, you did it, Mom."

Ginna even smiled sidewise at me. "Did he help you, then?"

I nodded. "Dave owns a cabin near the ski area, so we could cut a tree off his property. We brought it last night when I came home."

By this time, Danny was grabbing the tree from my hands. "Can we decorate it now?" I was glad he seemed too preoccupied with the tree to think about Dave.

"Of course. It's Sunday, and with Christmas so close—only three days—I feel like we should go to church this evening."

"We haven't taken Annie to church much," said Ginna. "Maybe evening will be better, after she's all fed and ready to sleep."

I reached over and patted her arm. "That's a plan then."

By this time Ginna had closed the front door, and Danny was getting the tree into an old stand. *I wonder how he found it so fast. It wouldn't surprise me if he's been keeping it in his closet just in case.*

Next the strings of lights came out, and thankfully most of them still worked. Danny was the one who produced the big cardboard box of ornaments, too.

"What are you, a magician, son?"

"Sort of. I've been hoping to decorate something this year. My bedroom is right next to the attic storage, you know."

The wistfulness in his tone made me want to hug any of his fears away, but all I could do was smile. At last I found my voice and added, "This is going to be our best Colorado Christmas ever, I promise."

"So you're not going skiing with Dave, again?" murmured Ginna.

"No, he's going with his family."

"Oh." Ginna looked down, grabbed a couple of shining ornaments and hung them on the tree. Then we heard infant cries from across the room, and she hastened to see if Annie was hungry again or needed a diaper change.

***

Somehow we avoided the topic of Dave and his family for the rest of the day. Seeing the tree taking shape, with many of our old family ornaments, brought back a lot of memories.

Some of them were happy, but others weren't, so I avoided saying too much. After I'd fixed some beef stew for an early dinner, we got ready to head for the little country church about six miles away.

While Ginna got Annie ready, she sighed, "It's quite a production taking a baby out in winter."

I shrugged, "I probably had it easier when you were a baby. It wasn't as cold in Texas."

Thankful the roads weren't icy, I set out with the two girls in the back seat, where the infant seat fit better. Danny rode up front.

When we pulled into the small parking lot, I was surprised to see the church's tall white steeple lit with floodlights from below.

"Wow," said Danny, "It looks like a giant Christmas tree."

"Sure does," Ginna added. "Thanks for bringing us tonight so we could see it, Mom."

I was glad they were preoccupied with the decorations because as we walked into the tiny plank-floored sanctuary, with its rows of polished wooden pews on either side, I felt uncomfortable and didn't want anyone to pick up on it.

In front, a decorated tree stood beside the altar, and above was a lighted cross. Seeing that brought all kinds of memories—of my childhood, of our life with Tim. *And here you are breaking the Big-A of the Ten Commandments—adultery,* a voice was accusing in my mind.

Once we were seated near the back, in case the baby fussed, I tried to occupy myself with reading through the service bulletin. We hadn't been here much since Annie was born. I noticed some surprised faces glancing our way, which added to my discomfort. *Here I am, the divorcee, with my unwed daughter.*

Trying to keep myself from jumping up and running out in panic, I glued my eyes to the front of the room, either staring at the tree or the pastor as he began his message. I didn't even remember singing the opening hymn.

When he began his sermon, my mind was doing that weather-vane again, swinging back and forth. But one thing he said cut through everything:

"Please remember that God knows we aren't perfect, that there's no way we can make ourselves right with him. That's why Jesus came, to be born in a humble stable, to live like the lowest of us, to take our sins upon himself. This is the one and only thing that matters, at Christmas or any time of year. Keep this hope, this Christmas light, in your heart during all the things life may throw at you."

Life had certainly thrown me some curve-balls. My eyes were teary even before the closing hymn began. As I sang the words, their reality burned into my mind:

> *The Lord is never far away, but thru all grief distressing,*
> *An ever-present help and stay, our peace and joy and*
> *blessing.*
> *As with a mother's tender hand He leads His own, His*
> *chosen band:*
> *To God all praise and glory.*

Like a mother. Those words hit the most. I'd lost my mother when I was younger than my own daughter was now. No wonder I wasn't very good at this role. And yet, the words I'd just sung reminded me God was more than a father, far away, disappointed, and angry. He was like a mother, too, wanting to comfort me and help wipe away my tears.

God, I'm sorry. Help me do a better job here.

We didn't stay to visit after the service because the baby was fussy. But the pastor warmly shook my hand as we headed out the door.

"It's good to see you and your family, Lauren. I hope you'll join us again soon." I was most surprised that he'd remembered my name.

***

The baby fell asleep on the car ride home, and Ginna was able to get her into the crib without waking her. Danny went straight upstairs, yawning. I turned on the tree's lights and sat across the room on our saggy couch to take in the beauty. Another reminder of my childhood, when I'd lie under our Christmas tree every night, staring up into the lights. I didn't let my mind move on to nights I'd sat with Tim on this very couch when it was new.

As I was closing my eyes to keep those memories away, Ginna came and sat beside me.

"Annie's asleep. Taking her out was a lot of work. I need to catch my breath."

"Looking at a Christmas tree is a good way to collect your mind."

"I'm glad you got it for us," she whispered. "I suppose it's nice that Dave helped." After a long pause, she added, "I saw you crying at church."

This brought tears to my eyes again. I still had a tissue in my pocket, so I swiped at them. "Danny knows," I murmured.

"Yeah, he told me. Mom, I'm sorry I've been hard on you. The more I face being a mother myself, the more I see how hard it is. And you have to be like a dad now, too."

"I'm the one who's doing a bad job, Ginna. Tonight I realized I should rely on God and not another man to help me, especially since that man is married to someone else. I've gotten myself into a mess that I'm having a hard time getting out of."

"I'm stuck in my own mess, Mom. Listen, I just want you to know that I didn't plan to get pregnant to spite you or anything. It *was* an accident."

There was so much more I wanted to ask her, but I held my tongue. Then an awful thought flashed into my mind like a bolt of lightning: *What if Ginna was raped right here in the house one of those times I left her alone so I could be with Dave?* My heart thumped against my ribs, and the room took a spin around me.

"Ginna, I'm so sorry." It was the only words I could muster.

She made no reply. I reached for her hand and gave it a squeeze. Tears dribbled down my cheek as we stared into the tree's colored lights in silence.

"I know what *I* need to do," I said at last. "But I'm just too weak to do it. Don't think I haven't tried."

"That night you had crumpled paper-wads all over the floor?"

I nodded through my tears. "That was the first try. Not the last. It's just that I've been so lonely."

"I'm sorry, Mom," she murmured. "I'll try to be here for you more. It's been hard with the baby and all."

"Thanks, I'll do the same." I squeezed her hand again.

CHAPTER 12
Ups and Downs
– Moving into 2009

We had a quiet family holiday. The tree filled the house with its fresh woodsy scent, which helped make up for the lack of presents under it. I had managed to get Ginna an inexpensive digital camera, with help from Danny in choosing the right one. It was her only real gift.

Ginna and I combined to get a gift for Annie–a new pair of pajamas, with bright red and white candy canes on a pink background. Annie tried to pull them over her head.

"Wow, she seems to know they're something to wear," said Ginna. "I'm glad she likes them."

When Danny's turn came to open gifts, I became anxious, wondering if I'd bought the right computer game. I was relieved when his eyes lit up and he cried, "Just what I wanted, Mom!"

The last package under the tree seemed lonely. "That's my gift for Danny," Ginna said.

He unwrapped the package carefully, as if to make the moment linger. At last, the box was opened to reveal a set of brightly colored markers.

"Wow, this is neat," he said, giving his sister a quick hug.

"They're good for drawings of all kinds," she said. "But don't let Annie near them. They're permanent ink."

"I'll keep them in my room."

"Yeah, she can't climb the attic steps yet, so that should work."

At the end of Christmas Day, once the baby was asleep, the three of us sat in the living room and admired the lights and ornaments on the tree.

"I'd say we had a pretty good holiday," I sighed. "Sorry there couldn't have been more presents."

"Don't worry, Mom," said Ginna. "That's not the most important part of Christmas, you know."

"Yeah," Danny added. "It's just being together."

I heard a catch in his voice and knew he was probably thinking of his father. We hadn't heard from Tim this Christmas, just like last year. For the first couple of years after we'd moved to Colorado, he'd at least sent a card.

To get my mind off Tim, I said, "Let's sing some Christmas carols."

"Good idea, Mom," Danny chimed in.

We started with *Jingle Bells*, each of us trying our best to sound merry and bright.

"What should we sing next?" Ginna asked. "How about *Deck the Halls*?"

This one further brightened the mood, and we followed it with *Joy to the World*.

"The church my parents went to always ended the Christmas service with that one," I added as we all stopped to catch our breath. "How about a more quiet one? I just remembered this one. See, I grew up in Texas, too, like you all. It never snowed for Christmas there, but we wished it would. My dad would always get out his old Bing Crosby recording of

White Christmas. It became our ritual to sing along with it just before we went to bed on Christmas Eve."

Even as I said this, my voice caught in my throat.

"That's a special memory," whispered Danny.

"How old were you when your dad died?" Ginna asked.

"I was fourteen."

"Younger than I am now," she murmured, looking past me into the tree's lights.

My eyes grew misty. "I don't think I can sing it tonight. Will you help me with *Silent Night* instead?"

Danny reached over and took my hand. "Sure, I remember it from church programs we did in Rusk."

I smiled ruefully. This whole evening was filled with bittersweet memories.

The kids started the song: "Silent night, holy night—"

I finally joined them at the end, "Sleep in heavenly peace."

Silence settled again, until Danny finally rose from his spot on the floor beside my chair and patted my shoulder. "Thanks for a nice day, Mom," he said. "I love you."

I could only nod through more tears.

Ginna had risen from the couch and was heading toward her bedroom, carrying her new camera. "Thanks for this. Now I can take lots of pictures of Annie."

"You're welcome, Honey."

When both kids had left the living room, I was able to let the tears have their way at last. The lights from the tree became blurry colored stars. Once the tears began to abate, I turned everything off, headed for my room, and prepared for bed. Looking out the window, I was surprised to see it snowing.

"Merry Christmas, Mom and Dad," I murmured to the falling flakes.

After I'd been back at work for a couple of weeks, with all the Yuletide holidays over, I settled into my usual post-holiday slump. Dave had been gone until early January, and we hadn't seen much of each other even after he came back. I wondered if he was tiring of me.

I tried to focus on my children instead. Annie was developing a personality and kept us all entertained. She'd also settled into a regular feeding schedule, which greatly improved Ginna's mood.

I even dared to think things would continue to calm down between my daughter and me.

Then one day in mid-January Ginna showed up again at lunch time with the baby. My face flushed in anger and embarrassment when Dave jumped up and greeted them at the breakroom door.

"Hey, it's great to see you two," he smiled.

I stayed at the table, wishing I could crawl under it. Why was she doing this? How had she managed to talk some neighbor into driving her again?

By now, Dave was holding Annie and bouncing her on his knee, sitting across the table from me. He even chanted an old nursery rhyme, "Ride a big horse to Banbury Cross—"

"I think I remember you doing that one with me, Mom," said Ginna.

All I could manage was a nod.

Then he stood again and lifted the baby high in the air, as she giggled and squealed. "Look how big she is," he laughed. "So big, so big."

At last, I couldn't stand it any longer. Leaving my lunch

on the table, I rose, stalked out of the room, and took refuge in my office. Almost half an hour went by before he came to my door, tapping lightly and waiting for me to open for him. Grudgingly, I got up from my desk.

"Are you still angry?" he asked softly, as he stepped into my office.

I looked up at him and nodded.

"Look, I'm sorry, Lauren. I didn't know you had a problem with this. I mean I like your daughter, and I feel for her being a single parent. The baby likes me, so what's wrong with making them happy?"

He stood frozen just inside the door while I returned to my desk and plopped down in my chair. "It's just awkward. I don't know what to say or do. I mean, Ginna's not your daughter. I hope you don't expect her to take your own daughter's place, now that she's going off to the West Slope to work. Is that what this is about?"

"No," he said, moving slowly toward me. "I just think Ginna needs a friend, and well—"

"And you think she needs a father-figure, I suppose."

He stepped back at the tone in my voice. "Maybe she does."

"You're not the right person to fill that role," I snapped, standing back up. "I know you aren't planning to marry me. All this will do is break my daughter's heart later on. She's been through enough heartbreak already."

I stepped closer to him and stretched on tiptoe to look taller. "What do you think you're doing? Trying to come between me and my daughter?"

Instead of replying, he grabbed my arm and pulled me toward him. Before I could protest, he was kissing me so hard, it almost hurt. Soon, his lips gentled, and he began rubbing his hands across my back.

"You're tense as rock again," he whispered into my ear. "Stop carrying the world on your shoulders."

I tried to protest, but his kisses smothered my words. He worked his hands down to the small of my back and pressed me hard against him. My insides felt like melting butter.

"Dave, please," I whispered against his cheek.

"Don't worry, I locked your door."

***

When I got home from work that day, Ginna had prepared hamburgers and frozen French fries for dinner. I was so thankful at not having to make a meal that I ate ravenously.

In spite of the meal, my anger with Ginna began to rise again. Perhaps I was really angry with myself, but mirroring it onto her.

"How could you do this to me?" I asked through gritted teeth, after Danny had gone upstairs, and we were washing dishes.

"Do what?"

"Come to my office again."

"What's the big deal? Dave likes Annie, and she likes him."

"He's not your father, and never will be."

"Why not? I can tell he loves you. Don't you love him?"

"I do, but that's the problem. Can't you get it into your head? He's married and nothing will change that. I'm just his mistress."

"But Mom—"

"You're living in a dream world or something. Here I am

trying to break it off with him, and you're getting him excited about being your father-figure."

"I don't need another father. I just like him."

"Well, it makes things a lot more complicated for me. You know I have a hard time resisting him. I need a man, but I'm not sure he's the right one." I looked down, my heart thudding in my chest.

Instead of replying Ginna looked at me in confusion. "I don't have a man in my life, either," she said at last.

"You're the one who got pregnant, so there must have been a man somewhere in the picture. If all of this—the divorce and the pregnancy, rape or whatever—has been so hard on you, maybe we should look into counseling."

"Mom, stop it!" she exploded. "I'm not crazy. Why do you keep suggesting this?"

"Look, I'm just worried about you, that's all. People go to counseling for many reasons. Your father and I did for a while, but it didn't help with his sexuality problems. Getting counseling doesn't mean you're crazy, or mentally ill. My worry is how you won't talk about the rape—or whatever it was. What am I supposed to think?"

"I don't need you meddling in my life. Just leave me alone." Ginna turned her back on me and stalked across the room. Then, putting her hands on her hips, she turned and shouted, "You get to have him all to yourself. Is that the way it is? Are you jealous of me?"

"Ginna it's not like that. I just—oh, I can't explain it. I'm so confused by all this. Just when I began to feel like a normal human being, he came along and stirred up emotions I hadn't felt since before the divorce. Then, just as I got a grip on myself again, you had your pregnancy. Dave was my only refuge."

"I just want a little part of him," she muttered, "But you're too selfish."

Before I could reply, Ginna turned and fled to her bedroom, slamming the door. I wasn't surprised when Annie started crying.

"Serves her right," I mumbled, as I finished drying the last of the dishes.

***

The next day at five, Dave came to my office with his usual, "How's it going?"

As soon as he said this, the floodgates broke on everything I'd been stewing over. I looked up at him and burst into sobs. He came around the desk and grabbed me into a tight hug.

"What's wrong? Is the baby sick?"

It was strange that he asked about Annie first, but I could only shake my head. All the while he held me close, wiped my wet cheeks, and kissed the tears away.

After my sobbing ebbed, he murmured, "Come on, it can't be so bad, if the kids are okay."

When I finally gained control, he had me sitting on his lap in the desk chair.

"It's Ginna," I muttered at last. "I'm really worried about her emotional state."

"Postpartum depression?"

"Perhaps. I don't know. She won't admit to being raped, and never has any other explanation for her pregnancy. When I try to suggest she get some counseling, she flies off the handle. I think she's in denial about the whole situation and losing touch with reality."

He stroked my back for a few moments before he spoke again. "I suppose this could be shock from a rape, if that's what happened."

"I know. But she won't let anyone help her."

Silence settled between us. I couldn't think of anything to say until I finally noticed what we must look like, both in my chair. "I hope you locked my door."

He smiled and nodded. "Just to be safe."

"Please don't try to seduce me right now. You know I can't resist you."

"Hey, I'd never take advantage of a damsel in distress."

I leaned into his broad chest. "That's one thing I really like about you," I sighed. "You care. I must admit, though, you are turning me on."

"Sorry about that. I do have a prior engagement."

"With who?"

"My daughter. She's moving into a new apartment in Glenwood Springs soon, and I'm helping her pack and load stuff she still has here."

"Oh, okay."

Instead of continuing, he began to weave his fingers through mine. "Your hands are so cold."

His hands were nice and warm, and his breath on my cheek was giving me gooseflesh. "So warm me up."

He rubbed my hands between his for a few minutes, but then he stopped. "I'm sorry, but I have to go. My daughter is expecting me."

"All right."

I was staring at the ceiling of my hospital room again, as my mind shifted away from these memories. A nurse had just changed out my IV bag. After checking my vitals, she said, "Would you like to try having some real food?"

"Sure, if you think I'm ready."

"I'll bring some pudding for a start. Any favorite flavor?"

"Chocolate, of course."

She returned a bit later with a small container. I was thankful she pulled the foil cover off for me. Even under normal circumstances, I had trouble with those things.

Having the food helped me take a break from the long chain of thoughts I'd been having. If fact, after I'd finished the pudding, I fell into a normal sleep.

When I woke, though, the memories continued rolling by.

CHAPTER 13
Out of My Hands - 2010

As months passed, I tried not to encourage Dave. I brought a sack lunch and my own coffee from home, so I could avoid the breakroom. At home I'd started reading my Bible again on mornings when I had the time. One day, I came across this verse in the book of Proverbs:

"As a dog returns to its vomit, so a fool repeats his folly."

It was an ugly thought, but it hit me that I was like that fool. I'd kept on letting Dave seduce me, even though I knew I shouldn't.

Perhaps God was preparing me for what came next, but I still wasn't ready when it did.

Dave had sensed my hesitation, I suppose, for he'd stopped coming to my office for a few weeks. One afternoon at five, I was surprised when the familiar knock came on my door. He stepped right in before I could react. Looking up from my desk and trying to be casual, I quipped, "Well, look what the cat drug in."

"That's a weird line," he grinned.

"My mother had a million of them."

"Sounds like an interesting lady. Is she still around?"

"No, both my parents died while I was a teenager. Remember?"

"Oh, sorry." His eyes showed their warm concern that I found so endearing. "Accident?"

"No, cancer."

"So sorry."

"It's all in the past now."

He moved closer to my desk. Something was different about him. He seemed quieter than usual, and put his hand gently on my shoulder, instead of running it through my hair as he often had before.

"Lauren," his voice sounded hesitant. "I have some news for you."

"Okay?"

He cleared his throat before he replied. "I've been offered a new job at a nuclear power plant near Sheboygan, Wisconsin."

"Where's that?" My heart began to race.

"It's north of Milwaukee, on the shores of Lake Michigan."

"I've never been to the Great Lakes." I hoped I wasn't sounding upset, though I was shocked. "What made you want to go there, with so many cities and no chance to ski?"

"Well, there are some ski areas in northern Wisconsin. I also like sailing. We used to live on the Michigan side of the lake, in Benton Harbor."

"I suppose there's a nuclear power plant there, too."

"Actually there is, also on the lakeshore."

"So is this lake lined with power plants?" By now I was being sarcastic to cover up my confusion.

"It's a huge lake. So, no. Although there are several."

"And I guess your whole family is moving back to this old stomping ground of yours."

"Except for our daughter. Her job is here in Glenwood Springs."

"Yeah, I remember."

He was standing right over me now, and I could sense he wanted to hold me, but I stayed glued to my chair. Moving his hand from my shoulder to my neck, he massaged it gently. "We'll find a way to see each other," he whispered in my ear.

I took a deep breath. God must have dropped this into my lap for a reason. I realized that ever since Christmas, my thought patterns had been changing.

So I said, "Uh, I think maybe we should cool it for a while, Dave. I need to pay more attention to my kids and their lives, not just my own."

He'd moved his hand to my cheek. I felt the familiar stroke with his thumb that turned me on. Trying not to succumb, I gritted my teeth and stood up.

Turning to face him, I stared into his gray-blue eyes. "When is this big move taking place?"

"In a month. That doesn't give me much time to sell our house here and hunt for one there."

"You know, it's funny, but I don't even know where you live."

"Yeah, I guess not."

"That's your secret—your other life."

"My house is in Fort Collins. I'm sorry if that bothered you."

I looked down at my feet. "No, I understand. It's ironic that you know where I live, though." I took a deep breath before I continued. "Dave, I don't think I can go on like this—not with you leaving. Please, just let me breathe."

"What's wrong with you today, Lauren?"

"I'm trying to sort my life out here. Give me some time. I mean, you've just dropped a bombshell on me."

He was reaching for my hair, but I stepped back.

"All right. If that's how you feel, I'm sorry. I guess maybe I hoped our love was strong enough for this."

"Strong enough? To keep me in limbo while you go on with your family life and use me for your plaything?"

He glared at me, shock in his eyes. "That's not how I feel at all."

"Well, it's how I feel. Just go back to your great lake and your sailing adventures."

Even though we were in my office, I stalked out and shut the door behind me. He probably came out while I was in the restroom, trying to collect myself.

We saw each other after this in the break room, but after a couple of days, I went back to bringing a thermos of coffee with my lunch from home, consuming them at my desk. He didn't come back into my office, which was a relief.

There was an office farewell party for him, but I only appeared for a few minutes to convey my so-called best wishes, slipping out as soon as I could.

After he moved, a couple of letters came from him, not to my house but to the office. I was thankful Ginna didn't see them, but was fearful of what my coworkers thought. After reading each one, I shredded it. I was still wondering how to answer them, when the third one came. It had a very different tone from the others:

Dear Lauren,

Since I haven't heard any reply from you, I can only assume you are hurt and angry with me. I can understand why. I just want you to know that I do still love you, as I always have ever since you first came to our office in Colorado. You're a hard worker and I admire your skills. I hope you know it's much more than that, though.

You are also a wonderful, caring person who deserves someone much better than me. I'm sorry I can't be that man for you, but I guess it wasn't in the cards.

It's possible that we may cross paths again, and I actually hope we do. Perhaps you don't, and I can understand your hesitation. I still love you, but I don't want to make promises that I cannot keep. If those are what you need, I hope you find them someday.

Despite all the pain I may have caused you, I hope you can find it in your heart to forgive me. And that we can somehow be friends.

Love, Dave

I was weeping by the time I got to the middle of it. Since I couldn't bring myself to shred this one, I folded it and stuck it in my center desk drawer, which had a lock. I never did figure out how to answer it.

***

The next Sunday at church, the pastor talked about the importance of parents bringing their children up to faith in the Lord. One of the Bible verses he quoted was from Proverbs.

"'Train a child in the way he should go, and when he is old, he won't turn from it.' That also applies to girls, of course," he smiled.

Just as I was digesting the implication of this for me as a parent, he added another quote: "'The fruit of the Spirit is love, joy, peace, patience, goodness, kindness, faithfulness, gentleness, and self-control.' That's from Galatians chapter five," he said.

Ginna glanced over at me, and my cheeks flushed. I couldn't meet my daughter's gaze, but looked down, as that word 'self-control' loomed in my mind. Soon hot tears were flooding down my face. She reached over and took my hand. Thankfully, Danny wasn't looking our way.

By the time the closing song ended, I was in control again. Still, I made a beeline for the door, not sure I could handle talking to people in my current state of mind. On the way home everyone in the car was quiet, except for Annie's babbling in her car-seat.

"Sheep, baa, baa, baa," she chanted.

"Yes, a sheep goes 'baa'," said Ginna.

"Wanna be a sheep, baa, baa, baa," Annie continued in a sing-song voice.

Dany turned to his sister in the back seat. "I think she's trying to sing *The Sheep Song*, Sis. Remember? We learned it one year at Sunday School in Rusk."

"Oh, yeah," Ginna replied. She broke into song and Danny joined her:

"I just wanna be a sheep, baa, baa, baa. And I pray the Lord my soul to keep…"

Annie was 'baaing' right along with them.

I couldn't stay focused on their singing, though, for my mind bounced around like a ping pong ball.

I'd put a roast in the slow-cooker before we left that morning, so dinner was ready when we got home. Thankfully. Once the dishes were washed, Ginna put Annie down for a nap, and Danny headed for his bedroom, saying he had homework to do.

I dropped onto the sagging couch and sighed. When Ginna came out of her room, she joined me.

"Are you all right, Mom?"

This was all it took for the tears to overwhelm me again. Ginna sat beside me while I sobbed, holding my hand.

"What is it?" she asked after a few minutes. "What's wrong?"

"I'm such a poor example for you." I could barely get these words out.

"No, you're not, Mom."

I shook my head. "All I've been thinking about is myself. I never should have gotten involved with Dave. I knew he was married, but he was so warm and kind. I thought there might be a future for us, but now he's moved away."

"Mom, please," Ginna held my trembling hand to her chest. "You were hurt by Dad's leaving us, by his—"

I shook my head, "No, don't say it. I used Tim as an excuse, but as a Christian mother, I still did the wrong thing. Some example I gave you kids. I was showing zero self-control."

We sat in silence for several minutes. I glanced toward the stairs, hoping Danny couldn't hear us. For one thing, I still didn't want him to know about Tim's homosexuality.

"I know you don't believe me," Ginna said at last, "But my pregnancy was a surprise to me, too. It had nothing to do with you and Dave."

Ginna handed me a tissue, and I wiped my cheeks. "Why can't you open up about that, Honey?"

"I'm sorry. I just can't, Mom."

My heart began to pound. "I don't know what to say, Ginna."

"Let's forget it." She turned away, and I could see confusion on her face.

"I'm sorry." I reached out and held her arm. "It's not that I don't believe you made a mistake. Who am I to judge that?

Look at the dumb things I've done. I want to turn my life around, now that I see the damage I've done to you with my selfish affair. Danny, too. He spends too much time up there on his computer all by himself. The sermon today made me realize the time has come to make a clean break from Dave. He says he wants to still be friends, but I don't think that will work. I'm too weak when it comes to resisting temptation."

"It's okay, Mom. That verse Pastor read from Galatians says self-control and peace and all those other things are fruits of the Spirit. They come from God. We can't grow them by ourselves."

I nodded and sighed, "I hope God will help me begin to grow the right kind of fruit—instead of what I've been doing. I know I'm weak, but the Lord is strong, so I'm going to lean on Him now. Will you pray for me?"

"Of course I will, Mom. I think there's another verse that says His strength shows up best in weak people."

"I've heard that. It's in Corinthians."

"We need to hang onto that verse." She gripped my hands.

That night when I crawled into bed, I lay on my back staring at the ceiling for a long time. At last, I began to pray, "Lord, please forgive me. Help me do the right thing for my children. Help me learn to depend on you for what I need, instead of looking for love in the wrong places—like I did with Dave."

As I dozed off, a voice came into my mind. It wasn't audible, but there were distinct words: "You need to tell Dave about Me."

***

I guess God was testing my resolve, for twelve months later, just as summer was finding its way to the high plains, I got a call on my office phone from that power plant in Wisconsin.

"How's it going, Lauren?" came the all-too familiar deep voice.

"Well, I'm fine," was all I could think of to say. "You?"

"We're settling in. My son wasn't thrilled about changing high schools in the middle of his sophomore year, but he's finally decided he likes the school here."

"That's good." What else was I supposed to say?

"How are your kids?"

"They're fine, too. Ginna adapted to being back in school and graduated. She has one friend who still talks to her, named Annemarie."

"Really! That's ironic."

"Well, not totally. She told me she named the baby after this girl."

"You're probably wondering why I called after all this time."

"You could say that. This isn't just to check up on us, I'm thinking."

"Not exactly. Although I do think of you often, Lauren."

"Okay—"

"My boss is sending me to a conference in Spokane, Washington that's about a big PR project you and I did while we were working together. I bet you know the one."

"The HTGR?"

"Yep, the High Temperature Gas Reactor. Will you come help me present how we promoted this new cooling system for reactors? The interest in using helium gas as coolant instead of water is growing. Other power plants want more information, not just on the technology, but on the PR. I know your new boss will let you come, because I've already talked to her."

"Have you now?" My heart was pounding. Was it dismay or excitement? "When is it?"

"In two weeks. Do you think that will work for you? I can set up all the travel arrangements from here. You can fly from Denver to Salt Lake City. I'll also fly there from Milwaukee. Then we'll be on the same flight to Spokane."

"Sounds like you have this rendezvous all planned."

"Are you angry with me?"

"Not really, I guess. It will be nice to get out of the office for a while. Ginna's found a good sitter for Annie when she needs one, so there will be no problem there."

"It would be nice to see you again," he said softly.

"Just so you know, I'm not planning on this being one final fling, Dave."

"Since you haven't replied to my letters that's abundantly clear, but did you get my last one?" His voice sounded plaintive.

Sadness welled up inside me. "Yes, I did. I'm sorry I don't know how to say what I want to tell you. Maybe we can be friends, like you said, but I don't see how it could work."

"Okay—well–I'll email you the travel plans. Guess I'll see you on a plane in Salt Lake."

My hands shook as I hung up the phone. Why had I let myself be tempted like this again? But maybe this was what it would take to finish things off—to close that door. I had two weeks to mull over what to say to him. Those words I'd heard in my mind many months ago kept haunting me.

CHAPTER 14

End or New Beginning? - 2011

I sat in the Salt Lake City airport and stared into space for most of my two-hour layover. Again, I re-read the text Ginna had sent so long ago, that first night I'd gone out with Dave Cameron. It had come when we were waiting for the elevator, but like the selfish mother I'd become, I hadn't read it until after we'd made love. So ironic, for Ginna had said:

"Mom, don't think you'll get back at Dad this way. You're the one who'll get hurt, not Dad."

Why had I kept this text so long? Perhaps to attempt assuaging my guilt? To distract myself from these thoughts, I stared at my watch. Only twenty more minutes until Dave's flight arrived. He would be on the plane when I boarded. My heart pounded with anticipation and excitement, mingled with a cool aloofness I hoped to maintain.

Things would be different now. Even though my body ached for him, I couldn't let myself be tempted anymore. Would my resolve waver? It probably would have been better not to see him again, but our supervisors had insisted we both present this final report on the HTGR project.

I have to make a clean break, I thought. *His moving to another office is a golden opportunity. Don't blow this, girl. The emotional turmoil of this affair is too much. It has to end here.*

Besides all that, I'd decided to share some things with him about my faith, my deeper self. Why did that always seem so hard to do? Probably because I was still hiding behind the hurt Tim had heaped on. *I should be over it by now, as my friends keep telling me. After all, it's nearly nine years ago. Maybe if he'd just left for another woman, it would be easier. And if he hadn't cut us off.*

Soon I was walking toward the jetway to board the plane, surrounded by a crush of people but alone in a crowd, enveloped in my own sphere of thoughts. No one around me could have guessed that soon I'd be seeing my former lover's face.

The crowd flowed down the corridor to the door of the plane. A smiling male flight attendant checked my boarding pass. I rounded the corner, walking through the first-class section into the coach cabin. Three seats to the left, two to the right. My eyes began to roam across the heads and stopped to the right, halfway back. There he was, with a smile and upraised hand. I nodded and moved to take the seat beside him. How had he managed to get our seats together?

"Hi," I murmured.

"How are you?"

"Oh, I'm fine." Glancing out the jet's tiny window, I searched for words. "How is your sailing going?"

"The weather hasn't been very good. I ran in a six-mile road race last weekend, though."

I couldn't help admiring his broad shoulders and chest. He was very well-built for a man in his fifties. And, yes—sexy, too.

Soon we started comparing notes on the presentation we were to give at the conference in Spokane. I'd carefully prepared, wanting to make a good impression.

"I just threw some stuff in my briefcase," he laughed. "We can put it all together later. I know you'll do great."

"You can afford to be that way," I smiled. "You're already a super-VP, not like little me, who's trying so hard to get noticed in the organization. Besides, your part of the presentation is the general stuff. Mine is more specific and detailed, so it has to be precise."

"That's why you have that part. You know, you're very good at what you do."

"Sure wish the higher-ups would give me credit for it. My new boss is telling me to settle down and just do my old job."

"You're kidding. Well, someday they'll give credit where credit is due."

"I hope so. Sometimes I get the feeling I got used as cheap labor on this special project."

"Sounds a little bitter to me."

"Well, I don't think I've been treated fairly."

"Just hang in there for a while. Things will change."

"That's all I can do, I guess. And I *am* excited about this presentation. I hope it goes well."

"With your thorough preparations, I'm sure it will, Lauren."

By this time the plane was on its final approach to Spokane.

At the airport, Dave, the seasoned traveler, took control and rented the car while I claimed my baggage. Apparently, he'd gotten by with just a carry-on. We both got a chuckle out of the car, an upgraded luxury model at compact rates, agreeing we weren't luxury car people.

As we left the airport and entered the freeway going to the west end of town, he reached over and took my hand. "You have such soft hands. Really nice," he whispered.

"Your hands are so big they nearly swallow mine up." I gently disentangled my hand from his grasp.

He laughed out loud, with the explosive sound I'd always enjoyed. Then silence settled between us like a curtain.

"I suppose I'm going to have to take a lot of cold showers," he grinned.

"Maybe me too. I'm sorry."

"Well, I don't want to hurt you. That's the last thing I'd ever do."

This was something I'd heard him say before. I still wanted to believe it. If he really meant this, then he'd be the most unique man I'd ever met.

When we arrived at the hotel, we each took care of our own check-in.

"Separate rooms," I muttered to the clerk.

"Yes, I have you right here, room 170 and 168. Is that okay?"

"That's fine," I nodded.

Soon we were wheeling our luggage down the hall. At his door, he paused. "How long do you need to get ready for dinner?"

"About thirty minutes."

"That long? What do women spend so much time on?"

"Hey, we have a lot of pieces to put back together."

He just shook his head. "I'll knock on your door in half an hour then."

When his knock came, I was still curling my hair, but opened the door anyway. "Come in. I won't be long."

He grinned as he stepped in.

"While you're waiting, you can open your birthday present. I know it's early, but I wanted to give it to you in person. It's kind of a parting gift, too."

As I finished my hair, I could hear him tearing the wrapping paper.

"Looks like a book of some kind," his voice came from outside the bathroom door. "Wow, where did you find this? I didn't think this version of Thoreau's *Journals* was still in print."

"It isn't. I'm giving you my copy. I know how much you liked his book, *Walden*. He's one of my favorite writers, too."

Suddenly he moved into the bathroom and pulled me into one of his bear hugs. "You are so amazing, but I hope you aren't really saying good-bye here."

"Watch out," I gasped as he tried to kiss me. "You'll get burned by my curling iron." This was all I could manage to say because my emotions were flying every which-way, the way my fine hair often did.

***

The first two days of the conference were stimulating. We were able to listen to the other presentations and discuss approaches to take with our own, which would be on the third day. The evening before, we worked on preparations in his room. I was uncomfortable with this, but the hotel conference room wasn't available.

"Isn't there some other room we can use?" I'd asked.

"Well, there's the bar," he laughed.

"No way I can concentrate in there, Dave."

"Yeah, I guess that leaves your room or mine. What's your choice?"

I'd opted for his because I thought I could muster enough willpower to walk out if necessary. *I can't very well walk out of my own room and leave him in there, can I?*

We spent almost an hour discussing our plans. I sat in the one desk chair, while he lounged in the easy chair in the sparsely furnished room. By the time we were done, piles of papers had been sorted, and a power-point was set up on his laptop. After he'd finished his part, he flopped on the bed, saying, "I'm bushed."

"Me too. I think I'll head for bed."

"Come on. Join me," he teased.

"Please, don't tempt me, Dave."

"I know you think you can't sleep with me again. But why?"

"There's no point if the relationship can't go any further. I'll always be the 'other woman' with you. My kids need more stability than that. I'm sorry, but I feel I need to set a better example for them."

"I'm sorry, too. Leaving my wife isn't an option right now. Why have you suddenly developed this guilty conscience? I don't get it."

"Dave, I can't be happy as only your mistress. I don't want to share you. There's no point in pretending anymore."

"I wish we could just live for right now."

"You know I'm not like that."

"Something's changed you." He closed his eyes. Soon he seemed to be actually dozing.

I gathered my papers and rose from the desk chair. "I'd better go now."

"I wish I could make you stay," he whispered, without opening his eyes.

"I guess you could. But you won't."

"No, I won't." He sat up and looked into my eyes. "Good night. What time do you want to go to breakfast?"

I was slipping my feet into the shoes I'd kicked off while we were working. "Oh, about six-thirty. Why don't you knock on my door when you're ready?"

"Okay."

He lay back and closed his eyes. It was easier to leave without his blue eyes pleading with me. "Good night, Dave."

***

The presentation went really well, and I was thrilled that the group responded enthusiastically. After the last session of the day, several of the participants went to the hotel's lounge for a few drinks, then dinner and dancing.

Friends from other cities that I'd met on the project were there, and I was having a great time dancing and reminiscing with them. Many complimented me on the presentation. I was glowing with pride and wondered if Dave noticed. But he seemed to be busy making the acquaintance of another woman from the Salt Lake City office.

I ignored this, telling myself it was stupid to let this hurt me. After all, if he wanted a bed partner, he had to look elsewhere. I'd made that clear. I knew he still wanted me, but I'd made a promise to myself to resist, and knew I had to keep it, if I wanted to have any pride left in myself.

As the evening ended, and the bar was closing, he suggested walking with me to our rooms. What could I say? His room was right next to mine.

When we reached my door, I smiled up at him. "I suppose you want a good-night kiss."

"Not out here in the hall where others might see, Lauren."

"Yes, I know." *Don't be foolish*, I told myself.

But, despite my misgivings, I opened the door. He closed it as he stepped in, gathered me into his arms and kissed deeply.

"You're still so special to me." He tilted my head back and nuzzled under my chin.

You should never have let him in, I scolded myself.

"I wish I could control my emotions," I mumbled as I stepped away from him.

"Don't try." He tried to draw me closer again.

"No, it's just the opposite. If I could control my emotions and not worry about tomorrow, I'd let go and say yes, But I can't, and I know it."

"Well, you're wise to know yourself."

"I think I'm finally beginning to."

"So I guess I'd better say good-night." He kissed me one more time. "You're sure?"

I nodded.

Then he smiled and opened the door. "Good-night, Lauren. I still love you."

"Me, too. But I'm not sure we can ever be just friends. Only time will tell."

"Is that another of your mother's sayings?"

"Uh—yeah, I suppose it is."

***

Very early the next morning, we checked out and headed for the airport so he could catch his plane. This time, mine would be a couple of hours later. I sat at a loss for words as we sipped coffee at a small café near the departure gates. After a few minutes of awkward silence, I knew it was time to act on those words I'd heard in my mind—the ones that seemed to be from God.

"Dave, I want you to know that I'll be praying for you, that God will work things out with you and your marriage.

Maybe he has a plan to keep you and your wife together, and that's why you can't leave her."

"I'm only staying right now because of our son," he said.

"That shows me what a good person you are. Not everyone says those things, so a lot of kids get hurt. Mine sure did when my Ex left us." I felt a sudden burning in my eyes and blinked. *Don't cry, silly. There's no point in that.*

"He must have been crazy to leave someone like you."

"If he and I had known the Lord the way I do now, maybe things would have been different. At least we could have prayed more about it. Maybe he wouldn't have decided he was gay. I don't know."

Dave reached across the table and grasped my hand. In spite of my efforts, the tears were beginning to trickle down my cheeks. "I wish there was more I could do. I'd try to help, if you'd let me."

Shaking my head, I stared at the tabletop. "I'll be okay. I know God loves me and has a plan for my life, even if I can't see it right now. I read once that someone said, 'I don't know what the future holds, but I know who holds the future'."

"Meaning your Lord, right?"

I nodded. "Oh, Dave, I wish you could know the Lord that I do. He really wants to come to you. The Bible says, 'He is not willing for anyone to perish'."

"Well, it's been a long time since I've been inside a church."

"I'm not really talking about church. I'm talking about letting God into your life."

"To save me from the mess I've made of my marriage?"

"Not just that. A savior from the mistakes all of us make. That's why he came, to save the world. But we each need to believe it for ourselves."

"Boy, that's a lot to take in."

"I know. I've been wanting to tell you this for a long time, because I love the whole person that's you, including your soul."

Swiping at my wet cheeks, I followed his gaze out the window where a plane was landing.

"When I die, Dave, I know I'll be in heaven with God forever. That's what he wants for everyone. It's like a gift that he gives, but we have to receive it." I paused, hoping he'd return his attention to me.

At last he looked back, and I smiled, pointing at the brown case on the chair next to him. "You could have just put my birthday present in your briefcase unopened. Then it would never have really become yours. That's what people do who don't accept what the Lord has done for them."

He squeezed my hand and didn't let go, but still said nothing.

"I'm not talking about just a few years, or even the rest of our lives here. I'm talking about forever—eternity. You know, when I get to heaven, I hope you'll be there, too. I really do."

He took a deep breath and finally spoke, "Well, I can't say for sure what will happen to me. I'll just have to do my best while I'm alive. I do believe in God, but I guess I don't really feel the need for a savior right now."

I gazed at him across the table, hoping that somehow he'd see the truth of God's love for him in my eyes. "I remember feeling that way, too. But someday, you *will* feel the need, and when you do, I hope you'll remember what I've said."

His eyes locked onto mine for a long time, and I didn't look away. Finally he smiled, "You are the most amazing person I've ever met. Do you know that?"

"You are, too."

Just then the loudspeaker announced the boarding of his flight.

As we walked toward his gate, he pulled me to him with one of his strong arms wrapped around my waist. "You're really special, you know that?"

"I'll never forget you, Dave."

I continued to follow when he headed toward the boarding door. His was a small regional jet, so he would be walking across the tarmac to the plane's stairs. We stopped at the desk by the gate.

"I guess this as far as I can go," I said. Somewhere in my mind, I could sense the double meaning of this. "Good-bye, Dave."

Suddenly he grabbed me and kissed me right there in the middle of the airport. "Good-bye, Lauren."

Then he turned, walked through the metal detector and out the door. I raised a hand to wave, but he wasn't looking back. The wind whipped his blue suit coat, and the sun made his gray hair shine. My throat was tight, and my eyes blurred as I watched him disappear into the plane. It taxied down the runway, and then hurled itself into the sky.

I turned slowly, not caring if anyone saw the tears streaming down my cheeks. In my mind, I said a prayer: *I guess it's in your hands, Lord.*

The boarding gate for my flight had just posted the departure time when I reached it. I had another hour to wait, so I sat down heavily in one of the black-upholstered chairs. Pulling out my cell phone, I stared at it for a long time. Finally, I pulled up my daughter's number to text her. At least now I could face Ginna. I'd listened to my conscience and done the right thing.

CHAPTER 15
Weaving A Tapestry

The day came at last when I was released from the hospital. I was taken down an elevator in a wheelchair to the main entrance where Ginna waited for me. I clung to her hand as we drove home in our little blue Toyota Echo, an older model, but the best we could afford. I tried to think of something to say to my daughter, but no words would come.

When we arrived at the house, I was so weary I went straight to my bedroom and collapsed on the bed.

"I feel like sleeping for a week," I said.

"Let me help you get comfortable, Mom."

"Okay." I was too tired to protest that I should be able to do something for myself by now. It had been just over a week since the surgery.

As Ginna pulled the shirt over my head and helped me into a nightgown, I avoided looking at my flat chest, heavily sewn with sutures.

"I guess I won't be needing any bras," I sighed.

"They make some for post-surgery," Ginna smiled. "I've been checking on the Internet."

"Where's Annie?"

"I left her at Grace's while I drove you. I'll go pick her up once you're settled. Grace sure is a good neighbor."

I nodded as Ginna lifted my legs onto the bed. My shoulders were too sore to help her get my sweatpants off.

Once I was under the covers, I tried to adjust the pillow. There was no possibility of sleeping on my side, so I fussed a bit about having my head in just the right position.

"Sorry to be so picky, Ginna."

"Don't worry, Mom. Love you much."

My mind was shifting into oblivion as Ginna softly closed my door.

I don't know how much time passed, but when I woke next time, Ginna was just coming into the room.

"Oh, good, you're awake. You slept yesterday away and today you've slept in," she smiled. "Let me help you out to the living room."

"I feel too weak to move, Honey."

"The doctor said to get you moving more, Mom. It's a beautiful sunny day, and it will do you good to sit out there for a change of scene."

"All right, if you insist."

"We've gotten some nice cards in the mail," she added. "You can read them while you relax."

Once I was settled on the old couch, I did feel better with the sunshine flowing over me. The cards said things about trusting the Lord and leaning on him. One talked about being in the hands of God, 'The Great Physician.'

"Lord, I know I need that," I murmured to myself.

Picking up another card, I read a story of a woman making a tapestry. A picture of the back of the tapestry showed a mess of meaningless threads and knots, but these made possible the beautiful scene on the front. Inside, the card read: "God's ways are as high above ours as the heavens are above the earth."

In blue ink the following words were added, "Remember, He promises to never forsake us. Let us know of any way we can help you, Lauren." It was signed by the pastor of our church.

"God," I murmured to myself, "I still don't know why you took both my parents so soon, not to mention all my other troubles. But I guess someday when I see the whole picture, I'll understand."

Another card had on its front the verse which had come into my mind that first night in the hospital, "Never will I leave you…" Its reference was Hebrews 13:5. Opening the card, I saw it was from Grace. She'd written, "I'm praying that the challenges in your life right now will lead to the blessings of a closer relationship with God."

"Yes, Lord, help me get through this," I sighed amid tears.

Reading this card from our neighbor set my mind remembering how she and I had met. It began shortly after I got back from the Spokane trip with Dave.

It had started with discussions about Danny wanting to buy a car.

One evening, Annie wandered across the living room while I cooked fried chicken. Ginna lay prone on the couch, hands over her eyes, nursing a headache. This was a common occurrence now that the baby was three.

"Hopefully some protein will help you feel better," I said as I walked past her, following Annie just to make sure she wasn't digging soil out of the houseplants again.

"I hope so, Mom," she mumbled.

"I turn on light," said Annie, pointing to the table lamp beside my favorite chair.

"Don't touch, sweetie." I grabbed my granddaughter's little

hand just as she reached for the green lampshade. We'd tried to toddler-proof this house, but Annie still found mischief. Nearly every day, I reminded myself, *this won't last too long.*

Now I led Annie toward the kitchen. "Come with Grandma. Let's get you a snack."

"Not too much, Mom. You'll spoil her dinner."

"I know. Just a couple of oyster crackers. They're her favorite."

Ginna turned her face to the back of the couch, away from the light of the window across the room.

Soon Annie was in her highchair with four of the tiny oyster crackers on the tray. She gulped them down in no time. Glancing over to make sure Ginna couldn't see, I added a few more. "Stay hungry," I whispered.

The chicken was almost done, nicely crisped. To make dinner quicker, I started some instant rice in a saucepan and put frozen peas in the microwave.

"Everything will be ready in ten minutes," I said. Walking over to the attic stairs, I called up to Danny, "Dinner's ready!" I knew he would take ten minutes to log off whatever computer game he was playing.

Having him isolated up there playing video games wasn't my first choice for family togetherness. *Sometimes you have to choose your battles*, I told myself. Now that he was sixteen and had a driver's license, his only other preoccupation was looking at used cars on the Internet. I often reminded him that he couldn't afford one until he got a good job.

I'd always hoped my kids could go to college, mostly because I never did. Tim and I had married right out of high school, and Ginna was born when I was nineteen. Back then, we hadn't felt too young—we were just like many of our friends in

Texas. If I had my life to do over again, I would've put marriage off until after college. As it was, though, going to college hadn't been an option for me, with both my parents gone.

Now Ginna's early pregnancy had put a damper on hopes for her, but I still had Danny's future to hope for.

Ginna was rising from the couch as Danny thumped down the stairs. "Not so loud," she moaned.

"Hey, I'm not loud," he protested.

"She has a headache."

"Oh, sorry." He sat down at the table next to the high chair and began making faces at his niece. I wished he'd spend more time with her, since he helped distract her from mischief.

"I'm going to get some more aspirin," mumbled Ginna.

"Isn't it too soon?"

"No, Mom," she snapped, stalking into the bathroom and opening the old metal medicine cabinet hanging on the wall.

Once all of us were finally seated, I led in our traditional mealtime prayer, "We thank thee, Lord, for this our food, for life and health and every good."

Both kids said, "Amen." Then another tiny voice said it, too.

"Good girl," Ginna smiled. "This is the first I've heard her do that."

With that as a start, the meal was pleasant until Annie started throwing peas on the floor.

"No-no." Ginna grabbed her hand as she lifted another few to toss. "Why don't kids like vegetables?"

"You didn't either at her age."

"I think it's the shape," said Danny. "Maybe she thinks they're little balls to throw around."

I was thankful he changed the subject, afraid Ginna was going to accuse me of giving Annie too many oyster crackers.

As soon as I took Annie's plastic plate away, she pounded on the highchair tray, chanting, "Cake, cake, cake!"

"What? Where'd she learn that?" Ginna looked at us accusingly.

I shrugged and turned toward Danny, who shook his head. "I don't know."

"Yeah, I bet," Ginna snapped.

"Shape up, you two. I'll get out the last of the ice cream." Desserts were a luxury in our house because of budget constraints.

As we ate the vanilla ice cream, I asked Ginna, "Is the headache better?"

"Yeah, I guess the food and the aspirin helped."

Once dinner was finished, I tackled the dishes. "Danny, it's your turn today," I said, running the hot water.

"Aw, Mom," he moaned. "I thought I did it last night."

"Nope, I did," said Ginna.

"Get over here, son."

He slouched to the sink and grabbed a dish towel off the handle of the fridge. Ginna began cleaning up the messy highchair tray and the peas on the floor. Then she took Annie into the bedroom to get her changed into her PJ's. At least, potty training was going well. She only needed a diaper at night now.

This house was really too small for four people, with only two bedrooms on the main floor and just one bathroom. Danny was making do with space in the attic as a third bedroom. I didn't like to admit I was looking forward to him moving out so we'd have more space.

After Danny had dried and put away the dishes, he headed right for the stairs.

"Wait a minute," I called. "We need to talk about something."

"What?"

"Come sit with me at the table."

He clumped back and slid into his chair. "Well?"

"You really need to look for a summer job this year."

"Why?"

"Well, I see you wanting to buy things, like new computer games or maybe even a used car. If you really want those, you need to start earning some money for yourself."

"Mom, that's not fair. You're not making Ginna get a job."

"That's between your sister and me. She and I have started to discuss it. Besides, she has a full-time job taking care of the baby."

"Always the baby," he snapped. "It's not my fault she got pregnant."

"And you're not paying the price she is, son."

He looked down. "Yeah, I guess so. It really wasn't my fault, you know."

"No one ever said it was." Was he going to feed me some fantastic tale, too? Ginna still refused to talk about how she got pregnant.

"While you're roaming around on the Internet," I changed the subject, "Try looking for job prospects in Eaton or Greeley. I know there's not much around here."

"How am I supposed to get to a job that far away? Walk or ride my bicycle?"

"Look, if you find some good possibilities, we'll look into the car sooner rather than later."

"Honest?"

I nodded.

"Okay. Thanks, Mom."

As he headed upstairs, I saw Ginna standing in the door of her bedroom, rocking Annie back and forth in her arms. "What about me? How come he gets a car? Just because he's a boy?"

"No," I snapped, a bit too harshly. Ginna turned and was about to close her door, but I added, "I have another idea for you, if you'll listen. Let's sit in the living room."

We moved toward the other side of our main floor, to the section we called the living room. It was actually just a couch and two chairs in one-half of the room that also contained the kitchen. My bedroom and the bathroom were off to one side of this main room, with Ginna's on the other. The baby's crib was still in Ginna's room, since there was nowhere else to put it.

Ginna sat down heavily on the saggy couch.

"Here, give me the baby," I said, settling myself into the rocking chair.

"So what's your great idea, Mom?"

Annie cuddled in my lap, smiling up at me. "Gamma," she said, and touched my cheek with a little hand. This was my favorite part of the day.

"Well, let's see, you're twenty now, so I was wondering if you should get a job, too."

"How am I supposed to get there?"

"I'm not finished here. Hang on a minute. I've just learned my job at the power plant is being phased out."

"Oh Mom, you loved that job. What will we do now? We need the money."

"I know. I'm hoping we can get by if both you kids are working. It will be tight for a while. Maybe I can get a night job somewhere."

"Okay, but what about babysitting?"

"I could do it for you, if I'm not working."

"Really? You'd do that for me?"

"Of course, I would. I think getting out of the house on your own will be a great change for you, Ginna. And I don't mind taking care of Annie."

"Does this mean I'd get to use our car? Danny might not be happy about your favoring me that way."

"Yes, I know. He's just going to have to learn to live with it. After all, he's a boy." I smiled, knowing I'd turned her negative comment about her brother on its head. "I'm hoping you'll be able to afford a used car eventually, too. It's possible both of you might find jobs that are close enough to ride together sometimes."

"Are you sure you want to be stuck at home all the time with no car? Some days it drives me bonkers."

Her words hit me like a bolt of lightning. *Now I understand why she's gone to the effort to find a ride to my office. I shouldn't have been so hard on her.*

I was ashamed to say this aloud, but knew I must. "Ginna, I'm sorry I criticized you for coming to see Dave and me at work. After all you've been through, babysitting is the least I can do for you. Maybe your job will have a schedule that will allow me to work evenings as a waitress or something."

"Gosh, that's a big come-down from being a key PR person."

It was true, but I didn't admit it. Instead I added, "I need a change of pace, Ginna." *And I'll be away from the haunting memories of Dave in that place.* I took a deep breath and added, "Of course, if Danny still wants to go to college, he'll have to get some kind of financial aid."

She stared at the floor at my mention of college, and I wondered what her hopes were for this. I wasn't sure what to say, and she didn't speak, so I let it go.

By now Annie was almost asleep. We sat in silence as I kept rocking her, humming a random tune. When the baby was sleeping, Ginna lifted her gently and took her to the crib.

She came back and took my hand. "You're the best mother in the world," she murmured. "Where would I be without you?"

"Oh, you'd manage. I know how strong you are, much stronger than I am."

CHAPTER 16
Life Goes On - 2012

The first year at home with Annie was the hardest for me. *Did I make a huge mistake?* I wondered often. Here I was, nearly thirty-nine, and some days I felt too old to be chasing after a toddler. When Annie took her afternoon nap, I usually collapsed on the couch and took a nap myself.

On one of those days, Grace happened to stop by. She lived about a mile up the road, closer to the highway to Eaton. Slightly perturbed at missing a much-needed nap, I still invited her in for coffee. We'd first met at the small country church. Talking one day after services, we discovered we were neighbors.

"How are you all doing?" Grace began, as we sipped coffee at the kitchen table.

"Oh, both kids are working, so I can watch the baby. What have you been up to? I haven't seen you in a long time."

"How old is Annie now?" she asked.

"She's three." I answered this question with hesitation, wondering what my neighbor's motives were. Was she here just to gather feed for the local gossip mill? I didn't know her well enough to be sure.

Almost like she read my mind, Grace's next words were, "Please don't feel like I'm interfering, Lauren."

"Okay—"

"You haven't seen me at church for a while," she went on,

"Because we've switched to a new and larger congregation in Eaton called *The Refuge*."

"Oh?"

"It's a very friendly church, with a lot of opportunities for meeting and socializing. My daughter particularly enjoys their Mother's Day Out Group."

"I'm afraid Ginna couldn't go to that if it's in the daytime. Her job is eight to five."

"Yes, I know," Grace smiled. "I was thinking of you."

"Me? I admit it would be nice to get out of the house once in a while, but I don't have any transportation. And I'm not the mother."

"My daughter says there are other grandmothers there. It's not uncommon these days, you know. I've been thinking of going myself, as a way to be with my daughter more. She lives over in Greeley now. I'd be glad to give you a ride whenever I go."

For the first time in ages, my heart lifted. "Really?"

Grace nodded and smiled. "I've been thinking of you cooped up here with that busy little girl. I guess the Lord put you on my heart."

***

Another year went by after this hope entered my life. Grace took us to the mothers' group the next week, and almost every Wednesday after that. Even when her daughter wasn't going, Grace still came by to pick us up.

Her generosity touched me so much that I soon moved my membership to *The Refuge*. Danny and Ginna didn't mind the shift, either, because there were more people their age in this new church. It wasn't that we disliked our little country church and its people, but we definitely needed the fellowship and support this bigger church offered.

Once I'd seen an old quote that said, "Is there life after forty?" Annie was nearing her fourth birthday when I turned forty. It was a tough birthday for me, with my mind saying things like, *Your life is half over. Have you accomplished anything?* My unanswerable question. And back then, I had no idea that cancer was on my horizon.

Ginna had found a good job in Greeley a few months after our conversation, right as my job at the power plant was ending. She was a secretary at a small law firm, and after her first year, they began training her to be a legal assistant. I was proud of my daughter's determination and diligence, for I knew that helped her get this promotion.

Danny's summer job that year was scooping ice cream at a touristy shop in Greeley. His hours didn't coincide with Ginna's, so they had to drive separately, which meant of course we had to find him an older used car to drive.

Now he was turning eighteen, and planning to go to college at the University of Northern Colorado, right there in Greeley. The owners of the ice cream parlor liked him so much that he was now their assistant manager, working every time he was out of school. I could tell he was excited about graduating from high school and moving onward and upward in his life.

Ginna's moods and headaches improved, too. Her work outside the home was a big help, but meeting other young mothers at church also opened some doors to friendships she needed very much.

Now that Annie was almost four, we were looking into possible preschool programs for her. Head Start was the best option. With her having a single parent and our low incomes, she qualified.

There were days when I still felt trepidation about Annie, though. One day after the mothers' group, she asked me a painful question.

"Gramma, who's my daddy?" She set her peanut butter and jelly sandwich on her plate as her blue eyes gazed into mine.

I'd often wondered how I would answer this question. "You don't have a daddy, sweetie."

"Paula at the church says everyone has a daddy somewhere."

"Who's Paula?"

"She was in my class today."

My heart sank as I wondered what to say. "Annie, we don't know who your daddy is—"

"Why not?" she interrupted.

This was going to be more difficult than I thought. Annie was a sharp little girl. I took a deep breath.

"Your mommy had something happen to her that she doesn't want to talk about. At the time she thought it was bad, but then you came along to make it all better."

"I did?"

"Absolutely, Annie. You're the little shining star in our lives. We can't imagine life without you."

She smiled and reached for my hand where it lay on the table. "Does that mean I'm good?"

"Of course you are."

"Paula said it was bad not to have a daddy."

"Well, Paula doesn't know our family," I smiled. "You have me and your mommy and your Uncle Danny, instead of just a mommy and a daddy."

"And that's better?"

"It certainly is, sweetie."

"I can't wait to tell Paula," she grinned.

Oops, maybe I've gone a bit too far. "Perhaps you shouldn't," I added. "After all, it might make Paula feel bad. You don't want to hurt her feelings, do you?"

Annie shook her head. "No, that's not nice."

"Then it's better not to say anything about this to her, okay?"

"Okay." Annie returned to the rest of her sandwich.

I told Ginna about this conversation when she got home from work that day. Annie was playing in the yard.

"Thanks, Mom. I've been trying to figure out what to tell her, because I'm not even sure myself how she came to be."

I flinched. Was the memory of her rape so traumatic she still couldn't face it?

"There's nothing I can say or do to help until you face up to this, Ginna."

"Mom, please!"

"Maybe you need to go to counseling."

"Not again, Mom!" She jumped off the couch and started toward her bedroom.

"Wait, I'm sorry. Please come back. I'm just concerned, that's all."

Ginna stood for a few moments, then stalked across the room and sat in the rocking chair opposite me. "Please," she began, "I'm all right, really. I don't need a shrink. I know you think I'm crazy, and sometimes I think this is all a bad dream. But somehow we'll get through it. I mean, there are lots of kids in the world who don't know who their father is, and they're doing okay. Annie will learn to cope as she gets older."

The slight desperation in her voice stopped my prepared curt reply about counselors. Instead I took a deep breath. "You're right, dear. Somehow the Lord will see us through this. He's the one who knows the plans he has for us. We don't."

Ginna reached over, took my hand, and squeezed it. "That's right."

That was all she said, leaving me with no idea where to take the conversation. We sat in silence until Annie came in from the porch.

"What's for dinner, Gramma?"

"Oh, I think I'll make pizza. Guess I better get started."

"Goody. Can I help?"

"You mean 'May I', dear. Yes, you may help with the dough."

"That's my favorite part." Annie ran toward the kitchen and pulled the flour out of the cupboard. "Let's go."

"It's hard to believe she's not quite four." I smiled at my daughter. "She's very bright and a quick learner."

Ginna nodded. "I know. The other day I heard her singing a song—I think it was 'Baa, Baa Black Sheep.' She was perfectly on pitch."

"I wonder where she got such a musical ear. Certainly not from me," I laughed.

"Me neither, Mom."

I never said any more to Ginna or Annie about it, but I wondered if her musical ability had come from her mysterious father.

After dinner and putting Annie to bed, Ginna went upstairs to her brother's attic room instead of joining me in the living room, as she usually did. The few times Danny was home, he kept preoccupied with his computer and rarely communicated with any of us.

This evening, however, I could hear their voices soon after Ginna climbed the steps. They were a low drone so I couldn't make out any words. Telling myself I wasn't really eavesdropping, I tried not to listen. The voices faded out for a while. Then came a loud thump, like someone had jumped out of a chair.

"No, Danny," came Ginna's voice. "I don't want to talk about it."

Their voices dropped in volume after this outburst. To hear more, I'd be eavesdropping for sure. I wondered if Ginna had opened up to her brother about what really happened to her, but also knew I would have to keep waiting for her to tell me the truth—if she ever did.

With a slight sigh, I rose from my favorite chair and went into my bedroom, getting ready for bed. That night, as I did my monthly breast exam, I found the lump in my left breast. My thoughts began flying everywhere: *Lord, what are you doing to me now?*

CHAPTER 17
Valley of the Shadow - 2013

It's nothing new, I kept telling myself. *You've had benign cysts before. Don't worry about it.* My annual exam with Doctor Thomas, our family doctor in Eaton, was only a couple of weeks away. *No point in rushing it,* I thought, hoping the kids couldn't tell how nervous I was.

When the day of the appointment arrived, I debated whether to get a babysitter for Annie, even though it meant spending extra money. Annie was almost four and could be trusted with the toys in the waiting room. The receptionist in this small doctor's office had assured me on my last visit, "It's no problem for her to wait in here. She's a sweet girl and no trouble."

Still, with getting a pelvic exam, I decided it best not to push my luck and got the sitter. It turned out to be a good thing. As soon as the doctor examined my left breast, his face registered concern.

"How long has it been since your last mammogram?" he asked.

"Almost a year. Why?" I tried to sound casual, but my pulse started racing.

"This needs to be checked out."

"Okay—"

"I see from your records that cancer runs in your family. Was your mother ever diagnosed with breast cancer?"

"She died from it." My throat was so tight I could barely speak.

"I'm sorry for your loss."

"It was over twenty years ago."

He raised an eyebrow. "Treatments have come a long way since then."

Turning to the countertop, he wrote on my chart. "I'm sending you to a specialist in Greeley. That way we can hopefully speed this testing up. With your family history, I'll go ahead and order an ultrasound along with your mammogram."

With Doctor Thomas's help, things moved more quickly than usual, but waiting was still tough. Fortunately, the specialist had an opening in a week.

Just a couple of days after that first appointment, my neighbor Grace had come over for coffee. As soon as I mentioned my situation, she offered to watch Annie.

"Oh, Grace, I don't want to put you out."

She took my hand in hers and squeezed it gently. "It's what neighbors are for."

When the mammogram date finally arrived, I dropped Annie off at Grace's on my way to Greeley.

"Lauren, you look pale," she said. "What's wrong?"

"I'm just nervous about the tests."

Grace pulled me into a warm hug. "I'll be praying for you," she murmured.

Tears sprang to my eyes. I turned my face into Grace's shoulder to hide them from Annie. "Thanks," I whispered. "For everything."

During the mammogram, I felt a sharp pain when the tech compressed my left breast. After this, the ultrasound was more comfortable, at least. I watched the fuzzy gray and black images on the screen, but they made no sense to me.

I was fighting back tears as I drove home, wondering if I should say anything to my kids. Somehow talking about it aloud made things even scarier, so I decided not to say anything.

When I picked up Annie at Grace's house, I nearly broke down but managed to keep it to myself because of my granddaughter. Grace looked into my eyes, but I shrugged.

"I don't know anything yet. Have to wait for my doctor to see the results. I'll call you later, okay?"

Grace pulled me into another of those hugs and nodded.

Perhaps Annie sensed something, too, because she didn't bombard me with her usual chatter as we drove home.

Sure enough, my doctor called a couple of days later to tell me he'd ordered a biopsy. Another trip to Greeley had to be explained away, but fortunately both Danny and Ginna were preoccupied. College was starting for him in only a few days. Ginna insisted on helping him pack for his dorm at UNC. My appointment at the gynecology clinic in Greeley the next week happened to coincide with his freshman orientation, so I could drop him off for the student portion and head for my appointment.

Ginna wanted to take off work and accompany Danny, but I convinced her to watch Annie instead.

"It will save paying a sitter," I told her at the supper table the evening before.

"What about our neighbor, Grace?" asked Ginna.

"She can't this time. Besides, Annie will enjoy having an afternoon for just the two of you."

"But I want to be there for Danny."

"Hey, it's all right, sis," he said. "It's mainly for parents and students, anyway."

She looked crestfallen, but nodded, "Okay, I get it."

I knew what my daughter's disappointed look meant. Ginna wished she was having college orientation, too.

"Maybe you could take Annie to the county fair, or something else fun, Honey. She'd love it." I was glad Ginna smiled at this idea.

That evening, I gave both kids a night off from helping with the dishes. It was easier to be alone with myself and my fears. I didn't call Grace until later that evening, when I could be alone in my bedroom.

***

The gynecologist's office was trying to be homey. Instead of the typical waiting room, this one had print-fabric couches and relaxing chairs to sit in. It looked more like the nicely decorated living room I wished I could afford.

Once they called my name, I was led to an exam room, with the usual table and pullout stirrups. I slipped into yet another skimpy gown, wondering if I'd have to live in hospital garb like this for the rest of my life. This thought made my heart sink. I was looking for a male doctor and female nurse to enter, when a single woman came in.

"I'm Doctor Perry," she said. "I'll be doing your biopsy today."

You shouldn't be surprised, I scolded myself. *This is the twenty-first century.* As I lay back on the table, my eyes were drawn to a bright poster on the ceiling right above my head.

"That's a good idea."

"You mean the picture for you to look at?" smiled the

doctor. "Thanks. Now, take deep slow breaths for me. This may hurt a bit. It's to numb you up."

There came a sharp pinprick, but then I didn't feel anything else except slight pressure on my left breast. In only a matter of minutes, the doctor was applying a bandage.

"We'll have the pathology report to your primary care doctor in a few days," she said. "He will call you with results. You'll get a follow-up letter, as well."

My heart was sinking at yet another wait. I made sure the hospital and the doctor's office had my cellphone number, since we'd recently dropped our landline to save money. Now that both Danny and Ginna had their own Trakfones, keeping the extra line wasn't necessary.

As I left the office and headed for the UNC campus, I took deep cleansing breaths to clear my mind. When I picked Danny up from his orientation, I concentrated on listening to his comments about plans for the future, instead of what the future might hold for me.

The call from pathology came six days later. Ginna and I had just moved Danny into his dorm. Grace wasn't available, so we took Annie along. She was in awe of the tall buildings on campus and stayed close beside her mother.

It was a warm fall day. Leaving Danny to settle in, we girls rested in a sunny spot on the grass of the college Quad. That's when my phone chirped.

"Is this Lauren Parker?" a voice asked.

"Yes."

"This is Doctor Thomas's office. We have your biopsy report from Doctor Perry."

"And?"

"It appears you have stage two cancer, which means it's moved into deeper tissue."

My whole body felt like it was falling over a cliff. Yes, I'd feared this, but hadn't confronted the reality until that moment. I was numb as I signed off the call, unable to remember anything else the voice said. What was I supposed to do next?

"Mom, what's the matter?" said Ginna, seeing my face. "Is something wrong with Danny?"

Looking at the shining green of the grass where we sat, I felt a tear in the corner of one eye. Somewhere off to the right, I heard my granddaughter singing, "Ring around the rosy..."

"No," I looked up. "Danny's fine. I have breast cancer."

***

They'd put one of those gauzy blue caps over my short blonde hair in preparation for surgery. Hair that I'd most likely lose anyway if I needed chemo. My hair used to have auburn highlights, but now they were silver-gray. *It doesn't really matter,* I told myself. But my 'self' wasn't convinced.

I lay in a cotton hospital gown, with what were supposed to be cheerful flowers on it. Usually these opened up the back, but for this surgery the opening was in the front. I put a trembling hand on my left breast. In a couple of hours it would be gone.

This shouldn't bother me, I kept telling myself, but it did. After all, I'd been carrying these boobs around for over forty years. They were part of my identity. Life was going to be strange without one of them—or maybe both.

In the midst of these thoughts, the surgeon came in.

"I'm Doctor Bailey," he said. "You remember we met last week at your pre-op?"

I nodded, making fists to hide my quivering fingers.

"We won't know for sure how many lymph nodes we may have to take until we get in there."

"Yes," I murmured.

"With your family history, a double mastectomy may be necessary."

"I know."

"It will depend on how the lymph nodes look. Do you understand?"

"Only too well."

"I see you've already signed for permission should this arise."

By now, I could only nod.

"All right. Your anesthesiologist will be in to talk with you soon. I'll see you in the OR."

Then he was gone, leaving me trying my best to breathe calmly. I reached down and felt both my breasts, and despite myself, thoughts of Dave came into my mind. I could almost feel his touch.

I shouldn't be thinking of him. But who else is there? Certainly not Tim. He never had much interest in boobs. Not surprising, with his sexual preferences.

The truth was, Dave was the only man I'd ever been able to turn to, the only one who fulfilled my womanly needs. No wonder it had been so difficult to break things off with him. He was still in my heart and mind. *Is he all I have to lean on in my present fears? No, you know better than this,* I told myself.

So, I mumbled a prayer, "Forgive me, Lord. Why do you seem so far away? I need you now."

Since my surgery was in Denver instead of Greeley, I'd discouraged Danny from missing his classes for it. I'd even told

Ginna not to stay and wait, so she could pick up Annie at the sitter's on time.

"Save your time off work for when I get home," I'd said. "I know I'll need you more then."

I was glad Ginna didn't ask for details as she dropped me off at the hospital's registration entrance early that morning.

Some people at the hospital may have wondered why no family came with me, but I thought it better at the time to be alone with my fears, not worrying about what my children were feeling. I'd be here at least three nights, probably more. The hospital would call Ginna to come get me when my release finally came.

Now, I wondered if I'd made the right choice. All I had left was a memory of Dave, hiding in the recesses of my mind, offering only a semblance of comfort. I'd never realized before how much human presence meant. Or how much I loved my children.

A nurse came in with a little pill packet and a small paper cup of water. "The doctor ordered this to help calm you," she smiled.

"Valium?"

"Similar, yes. First, please tell me your name and birthdate."

I gave them and took the white tablets with no protest.

My mind was beginning to get fuzzy when the anesthesiologist came in, so I couldn't remember what he said. A nurse came soon after, checked the plastic bracelet, asked my name again, then took hold of the bed and wheeled it into the hallway.

Another person joined, as we pushed through large metal doors with some kind of lettering on them. The last thing I remembered was reaching out and grabbing someone's hand.

What seemed seconds later, I woke to a blood pressure cuff squeezing my arm.

"How are you feeling?" came a gentle voice.

"Blurry."

"Are you in pain?"

"Not yet."

"Just press this red button when you need anything."

"Okay."

I wanted to look down and see what my chest looked like, but my head didn't want to move yet. The person was gone before I could ask any questions. I wasn't even sure if it was a man or a woman.

Closing my eyes, I waited for the pain to come.

It did, waking me from a stupor. Searching through the covers on top of me, I finally found the handset and pressed the red button.

A response seemed to take hours, for my sense of time hadn't returned yet. Instead of a pill to swallow, the nurse added something to the IV bag hanging behind my shoulder. Soon a cool relief flowed into my body.

When I opened my eyes to say thanks, no one was there. I tried to see more than the white blanket on top of me and the pale green curtain hanging to my left, but everything else was still fuzzy. I closed my eyes again.

The next time my eyes opened, the green curtain was gone. Instead I saw a window looking out on a view of Denver. On my right, someone reached over and took my hand.

"Mom, how are you?" The voice was familiar, but who was it?

As I turned my head, it felt as heavy as lead. At last my eyes focused on my son. "Danny? How did you get here?"

He smiled. "I drove over after my last class."

"Class?"

"At college in Greeley."

"Oh, yes." I tried to nod, but it hurt too much. "I'm still fuzzy-headed. The anesthetics must be hanging on."

"The nurse told me that could happen, Mom."

I squeezed his hand, trying to sense it better.

"Did the doctor tell you anything?"

"He hasn't been by since I came."

"Oh. Maybe we should call the nurse."

"I'll go down to the nurses' station and ask if they know anything," he said.

I nodded and let go of his hand. He seemed gone a long time, but the hands on the wall clock across from the bed hadn't moved much when he returned to the room.

"They said he'd be making rounds in the next hour."

"That's all?"

"I guess they have to let the doctor do the talking about the surgery."

"Yeah, I suppose so."

Weariness was sweeping over me, and my chest felt like a heavy weight was sitting on it. Closing my eyes, I clung to Danny's hand.

"Mom?" His voice came from far off. "Are you awake? The doctor's here."

"What?" My eyes popped open. "Was I asleep?"

"Yes," came another voice, probably Doctor Bailey's. "That's good for you."

"Did you take them both?"

"Yes. Lymph nodes showed the cancer beginning to spread, as we suspected."

"What does that mean?" came Danny's voice.

"She's still Stage Two," said the doctor. "We'll start with radiation to try and prevent it from progressing to other organs."

"Is that Stage Three?" I could hear my own voice, but it sounded strange and distant.

"Yes, if it's spread to other organs we call it Stage Three Cancer."

"What about chemo?

"Once you've regained some strength from the surgery, your oncologist will determine the value of that option."

"More waiting," I sighed.

"All of life is a waiting game." The doctor patted my arm.

As he left the room, I mumbled to myself, "Waiting for death."

"What did you say, Mom?"

"Never mind."

Danny returned to the chair on my right and took my hand. "I can stay a half-hour longer," he said. "But then I have to get back to school and homework assignments."

"That's okay," I murmured. "I don't want you to let your schoolwork suffer because of me."

As I drifted in and out of sleep, I felt his hand in mine and heard his soft breathing. Until the last time I woke. The scene outside the window was dark, except for the city lights. The hospital room was dimly lit and empty. I was alone with my ghosts and my fears.

"Lord, are you here?" I prayed. "Can *you* hold my hand?"

For a few minutes, I lay staring at the ceiling. Then a strange warmth came over me. A voice in my mind whispered, "Never will I leave you. Never will I forsake you."

CHAPTER 18
Settling in at Last — 2013 Into 2014

After a couple of weeks, I gradually regained some strength and did my best to take care of myself. Things like getting out of bed and dressing became major accomplishments. Making toast or pouring cereal for breakfast were breakthroughs. Each baby step gave me a sense of satisfaction, for this was freeing Ginna to go about her own life.

Annie was four and a half years old now, and took delight in being Gramma's helper. I gave her some special tasks, such as bringing books to read from the shelf behind the kitchen door. We didn't have any other place to fit a bookshelf in our tiny house.

Whenever the sun shone bright through the main window in the living room, I'd see dust motes flying in the air and settling on the furniture. Soon Annie had another job, dusting with a green feather-duster.

Three weeks after my release from the hospital, my first trips to radiation therapy began. This time the drive was to Fort Collins, which was closer than Denver and had less heavy traffic. It still felt like the big city compared to Deer Path. Ginna often brought Annie so they could go shopping at the mall while I was in the radiology department.

It would have been nice to join them, but the radiation

left me feeling so chilled and worn out that I didn't have the energy. Once Ginna picked me up, we drove straight home, and I crawled into bed. Occasionally, I felt strong enough to curl up on the couch with a fleece blanket wrapped around me. Annie adapted to these times by reading one of her *Little Golden Books* aloud for me.

"She's really reading these," I told Ginna one day.

"Oh, I doubt it," she responded. "We've read them to her so many times that she's got them memorized."

I nodded and didn't argue. One day, though, I turned to a page in the middle of a book we hadn't read in weeks and asked Annie to tell me what certain words were. She didn't miss a one.

I began to feel human again. Christmas came and went without much hoopla. With the mounting medical bills, there were few presents under the tree this year, but we were used to making do with what we had.

Danny came home from UNC for a couple of days at Christmas, but went back as soon as his dorm reopened. Even when he was home, he acted distant. I wondered if anything was wrong but was afraid to ask. Perhaps it was his way of coping with the cancer. At least Ginna and I were getting closer.

Right after the holidays, my oncologist, Doctor Jensen, met with me at her office in Greeley, where we discussed the plans for chemotherapy.

Again, I would be able to go to Fort Collins instead of Denver. To start with, the treatments were twice a week, then would drop to once a week after the first month.

"I want my daughter to get back to a normal work routine," I said to the doctor as we looked at this schedule. "We really need the income. And I don't want my son to mess up his college classes at UNC."

"Well, there is a shuttle service that runs from Greeley each Monday and Thursday. Perhaps we can get your treatments scheduled to fit."

"That would be wonderful. My daughter could drop me off on her way to work here in Greeley."

"And your granddaughter?"

"She has Head Start each weekday morning beginning at eight. It lasts until 3:30."

"The shuttle will be bringing you back here at two p.m."

"Maybe my son can meet me at the shuttle, if he doesn't have class then. I could stay at his dorm until Ginna gets off work to come take me home, once she picks up Annie."

All this did finally fall into place, though Danny had to drop a class that met at two on Tuesday and Thursday.

"Oh, Danny, I'm sorry you had to do that. Wasn't there any other time to switch to?"

"No, Mom. The other section was full. Hopefully, I'll fit it in next semester, when you're all better."

I wanted to smile at his optimism, even though I didn't feel any yet. Looking at my flat and empty chest in the mirror was still depressing. Some days I scolded myself for being so negative. Wasn't life more important than anything else? But I worried about how much impact all this ordeal was having on the lives of my children. Perhaps I was pessimistic because of what I'd gone through with my own parents.

For the month of January 2014, Ginna took me to the shuttle stop each Monday and Thursday, after she'd dropped

Annie off at Head Start. In February, the day shifted to just Thursday.

I enjoyed seeing my children during these times. Ginna, Annie, and I could visit while the three of us drove to Greeley. Then I was able to spend more than an hour with Danny at his dorm while we waited for Ginna to retrieve Annie and come for me. Danny began to open up a little during these times.

"I'm afraid, Mom," he said once. "I lost Dad, and I don't want to lose you, too." The look in his eyes told me this fear was one reason he'd withdrawn from me.

I was uncertain what to say, since I had no idea yet if these treatments were going to help me heal or not. I wished I could have said more and opened a deeper conversation with him, but this was the only time he said anything about it.

Most other times in the dorm, he did school work while I read a book. But at least we were together. Sometimes I also sensed anger in his fear. Was it directed at me? Maybe he still resented my affair with Dave. Or was he angry with God for allowing the cancer?

The biggest problem—besides the expenses, of course— was the nausea and diarrhea caused by the chemo. There were days when I wondered if the strong chemicals were killing *me* instead of the cancer.

Ginna tried to help by looking up possible herbs to give relief. I was surprised how much information she could find on her smartphone. It seemed like a miracle from the old Star Trek shows I'd watched as a kid. I remembered them 'talking' to the ship's computer and it answering in a pleasant female voice. It was so futuristic back then. Now my daughter was doing it in real life. Even my granddaughter knew more about computers and smartphones than I did, and Annie hadn't even started kindergarten.

After the first three months of chemo, I began to feel better. I could walk around in the backyard, and even managed to help Annie and Ginna plant a small vegetable garden.

We were blessed that year with a warm spring and a mild summer without any oppressive heat. The garden flourished, but so did the weeds. Sometimes, I went out with Annie to pull some of those weeds, while Ginna and Danny were at work, though I didn't have the strength to work for more than twenty or thirty minutes.

Then my granddaughter and I would head back indoors during the hottest part of the day and occupy ourselves with reading. At times, I'd take a nap on the couch, and often woke to find that Annie had drawn me a picture, sometimes with a story she'd written about it. The child's spelling was inventive, but she got her point across.

"I'm glad we can start her in kindergarten this fall," I told Ginna often. Whenever I showed her Annie's works, my daughter was surprised.

"Did I do stuff like this when I was four years old?" she asked.

"To be honest, I don't remember," I sighed. "I'm sorry. I guess I was overwhelmed with Danny when he was a baby, and your father—"

My voice broke at the thought of Tim, even now.

Ginna took my hand. "Hey, that's all past now, Mom. Don't worry about it. I know you did the best you could, and now I understand why Dad was so distant with us, because of his 'friends.' Danny and I love you for all you've gone through for us. Where would we be without you?"

Tears were spilling from my eyes by now, and I let Ginna give me a long hug.

In late spring, when Annie was only four months from her fifth birthday, I'd gathered the strength to take her to kindergarten screening at the local elementary school. The teacher doing the tests agreed that Annie was indeed ready for kindergarten. Even though her fifth birthday would fall after school started in the fall, she was deemed eligible.

That day had been worth the work it was for me, even though I was weakened and sickly for the rest of the week.

***

Fall roared in that year with a lot of wind, clouds and rain. Ginna wakened Annie by six a.m. each day in order to get her to the school bus stop on time. Danny was overloaded with his classes, trying to make up the one he'd dropped because of my chemo, so he spent most of his sparse home time on his computer. I wished there was more I could do for them, but my stamina was waning again.

When I was able to get an appointment with the oncologist, Doctor Jensen assured me that setbacks like this weren't uncommon with the type of chemo I was taking.

I sat in the doctor's office fighting back tears. "I want to be there for my children. They've had to give up so much for me."

The doctor reached over and patted my arm. "They're only giving back the love you've given them for all these years."

I nodded at her and smiled a little.

"I have seen articles on a new chemo drug," Doctor Jensen added. "I think it's worth a try in your situation. We'll just need to run a few tests to be sure you meet the criteria for a trial."

"A trial? Sounds like going to court with my ex-husband."

We both chuckled. "No, a medical trial. If you're willing to consent, that is."

"Might as well. I don't have anything to lose that I'm not going to lose eventually, namely my life."

"Well, we hope that's later rather than sooner," the doctor nodded. "Let's get started on this paperwork."

CHAPTER 19
Hope Arises

The new trial drug, Tucatinib, involved a long process. I sat two and a half hours each week, with a tube feeding into the port they installed in my upper arm.

The nurses or aides tried to make the time as pleasant as possible by having magazines available to peruse, and snacks to munch on. Sometimes I felt like eating, but not often. The fears of nausea were too deep after my experiences the first time around. I mainly sipped cool fruit juice and tried to focus on the gaudy and glamorous pictures in the women's magazines. How ironic to have cancer patients looking at images that were completely out of reach for them. After the first couple of sessions, I brought a book from home to read.

Now I was going to Denver, because this was a pilot treatment program. The drive was longer, but at least there was still a shuttle available from Greeley, though it was very early in the morning.

"I'm sorry, Ginna," I said every Wednesday morning as we set out at five a.m. She was carrying her sleepy child. "I hate to bother Grace this early, and I wish I wasn't such a burden on you."

By this time, Annie was secured in her booster seat, and we were wending our way toward Greeley. Soon the child was fast asleep again.

"Mom, you aren't a burden," said Ginna from the driver's

seat as we turned onto the main highway. "Just think of all the help you've given me since Annie was born. This is my chance to return the favor."

"If only this hadn't happened. Why did cancer have to run in my family? Now you'll have to worry about it, too."

"Mom, don't go there right now. There's no point in worrying about a future that may not come."

"All right. I'm sorry. Guess I'm just in a pity-party mindset today."

Ginna drove in silence for several minutes. The headlights of her car bathed the road in light, but beyond them and on either side, the darkness lurked, like it might reach into the car and grab me.

"I get such strange, frightening thoughts, especially when it's dark," I murmured.

"Maybe it's a side effect of the chemo, Mom."

"If it is, I hope it fades soon."

"I found a verse in my devotions yesterday that might help," said Ginna. "Romans 8, verse 28: 'And we know that in all things God works for the good for those who love him.' Somehow, this will work out, Mom."

"Thanks, Ginna. I know that's true, but sometimes my heart doesn't listen to my mind."

She reached over and squeezed my hand. "Mine, too."

This trial chemotherapy took a bigger toll on me physically. Again I had to depend on my daughter and granddaughter for help. Annie was a quick learner, though. Soon she was able to fix a box of mac-n-cheese all by herself. Warming a can of soup was no trouble, either, once we got an electric can-opener for her to use. Grace found one at a garage sale and was grinning from ear to ear when she brought it over to us.

One Saturday morning when I managed to get myself out of bed, I was surprised to see Ginna teaching Annie how to make pancakes.

Earlier that week, Grace had come by to see how I was doing. I'd been lying on the couch, so Annie answered the door.

"How are you?" asked Grace, as she walked in.

I could hear the concern in her voice, even though she was smiling.

We talked for about half an hour, but soon I was nodding and yawning.

"I'd better let you rest, Lauren."

"I'm sorry. This chemo is wiping me out."

"We'll pray it's wiping out the cancer, too," Grace took my hand and squeezed it. "I'll bring some supper by later."

"Oh, you don't have to bother, Grace."

"It's the least I can do," she smiled, still holding my hand. "Besides, all I need to do is double our own dinner recipe."

Before I could say anything else, Grace rose and moved to the front door, letting herself out.

Beginning that day, Grace came over with a casserole two or three times a week. This was plenty, since each dish she brought fed us for two days.

After about ten weeks on the new chemo, my oncologist ordered some tests in Denver to see if the cancer was regressing. Fear descended on me as I awaited the results. I kept on praying, though, and tried to trust.

Ginna found another Bible verse for me to hang onto, Jeremiah 29:11-

"'For I know the plans I have for you,' declares the Lord, 'plans to give you a hope and a future.'"

"I just love that verse," Ginna said on the day she drove me to the oncologist's to get the results. "Whatever happens, God has a future for us. I remember you said something like this to me when Annie was little."

I nodded and smiled. "Yes, you're right. Our future is either here or in heaven, I suppose."

"I pray you have more years with us here, Mom."

"Me, too, Gramma," added Annie from the back seat. We both were surprised she said this. *Young ones pick up more than we realize*, I thought to myself.

I was glad Ginna could bring her daughter along today because we hoped to have lunch at a favorite café in Larimer Square. Maybe—just maybe—it would be a treat to celebrate my progress.

Once I heard a verse that said something about praying without ceasing. That's what I was doing as we parked the car, took the elevator to the doctor's office, and settled in the waiting room after checking in.

The room was pleasant enough, with bright paintings on the walls and a corner with toys for children. Annie settled herself beside me with a book instead of heading for the toys.

"She really likes to read," I smiled at Ginna.

"Thanks to you, I think."

Annie had read two Disney storybooks to us by the time my name was called. I gave Annie a hug and Ginna grabbed my hand as I stood.

"Are you okay to go by yourself, Mom?"

"Yes, I'm feeling fine today." I didn't add that I wanted to process whatever the news was alone first.

The nurse took my vitals and then left me in the exam room. I tried to keep from wringing my hands while waiting for Doctor Jensen. When she entered the room at last, I could tell by her smile that my fears were relieved.

"Lauren, the tumors in your lymph nodes have shrunk. You're our new poster child for this treatment."

I was dumbfounded for a few moments. "Really?" I finally managed to say.

"This is one of the best outcomes we've had so far with this trial chemo."

"Praise the Lord," I murmured.

"Yes, that's what we can do," the doctor smiled.

It was good to hear this comment from her. Religion was a topic we'd never discussed. *Perhaps I should be more open about my faith.*

"What step do we take next, Doctor?"

"At this point, we wait and see. You will be off both chemo and radiation. We'll monitor you every other month for the next year. If there is no new cancer, then we'll be able to drop that to every six months."

"Life is always a waiting game," I mumbled.

"What's that, Lauren?"

"Oh, something I think the surgeon said after my mastectomy. But this was worth waiting for. I can't wait to tell my children."

"Just remember, though, cancer is a tricky beast. Remission can last for years, though the cancer may crop up again. A forever cure is not in the cards for anyone."

"I know. There's no cheating death. I just pray my end is farther off than it was a few months ago." I looked into the doctor's eyes and added, "One thing I do know, though. Even when I die, that's not the true end."

"You believe in an afterlife?"

"Yes, thanks to my Lord, I have heaven to look forward to, even if the cancer comes back."

"I'm happy for you." Doctor Jensen rose and patted my shoulder. "Having hope is one of the most powerful medicines I know."

CHAPTER 20
Riding the Wind Into 2015

The next year passed in the most normal manner of any I could remember since the divorce. Annie graduated from kindergarten and moved on to first grade. I'd always thought it strange to have a full-blown ceremony with little caps and gowns, just for kindergarten. But as I saw my granddaughter's beaming smile, I realized this small rite of passage was important in its own way. It was the opening of a door to the future, the life she would find as she journeyed through her school years, all the way up to the next rite, high school graduation. I prayed I'd live to see that.

Ginna's job at the law office in Greeley was giving her great satisfaction, too. "I feel like I'm doing something that makes a difference," she told me. "When I do research for the lawyers, I'm helping someone who is in trouble, even if it's just a neglectful landlord."

"I'm happy for you, and I feel good about what I do, too. My being here for Annie after school helps you concentrate on your work."

"Mom, I don't know where I'd be without your support. Probably having to deal with one of those bad landlords myself."

Christmas that year was our best one since Tim left. We weren't accustomed to a load of presents under the tree and relied more on home-made gifts for each other. Those had the most meaning anyway, because of the time and love that went into them.

One of the best surprises this year was when Danny brought a girlfriend to spend Christmas with us. They'd driven up in the little used Honda Civic he'd gathered enough funds to buy.

"It's Uncle Danny," cried Annie, jumping up and down by the window. "Who's that with him?"

Following her pointing finger, I saw a girl with red hair getting out of the passenger side. The Great Plains breeze sent her long hair flying, but she didn't seem to mind. Instead she reached for Danny's hand as they started for the front porch.

Annie was out the door before I could stop her, throwing herself into Danny's arms. I was busy noticing how tall he'd grown. His light brown hair was longer than before, but the waves looked good on him. My son had grown up while I wasn't looking.

When he stepped through the front door, he was still holding the girl's hand, while Annie clung to his other one. The first thing I did was give him a big hug.

"Mom," he smiled. "You look so good."

"I feel good, too."

"This is Sandy," he nodded toward the girl. "She and I have been dating since September. Her family lives in Kansas, but it was too far for us to drive there this year."

My heart began to thump. If he wanted to meet her parents, this must be serious. Disappointment welled up in me as I wondered why he'd taken so long to tell us about her. I'd hoped since my remission that he would draw closer again, but now it seemed he'd done the opposite.

For a while, I'd even worried he might be gay like his father, since he rarely talked about dating. At least that didn't appear to be true. Taking a deep breath, I shook Sandy's hand and smiled.

"Welcome to our humble abode, Sandy. I know you haven't traveled that far, but can I get you anything? Some coffee or hot cider perhaps?"

"Oh, Mom, you know I love your spiced cider," said Danny.

"I'd like to try some, too," smiled the girl.

Annie couldn't restrain her enthusiasm any longer. "Come on to the kitchen," she cried. "I can help Gramma make it."

"Wow, someone is getting very grown up." Danny, grinned at his niece.

While I poured the cider into a pan to warm, Annie pulled out the needed spices from the cupboard. Cinnamon, nutmeg, and cloves. She measured them carefully, just as I'd taught her.

"How old is she now?" Danny asked as we worked.

"I'm six years old," Annie piped up before anyone else could speak.

"And most precocious," I added, winking at my son.

Once we were all seated at the kitchen table with mugs of cider, Sandy smiled. "This reminds me of holidays at my grandparents' farm, an old-fashioned Christmas."

Danny patted her hand, which was lying on the table between them.

"Mostly, it's Christmas on a budget," I said.

"I think it's wonderful to focus on the simple things," said Sandy. "Like family, love, and friendship. That's what Christmas is truly about."

"And Jesus's birthday," added Annie.

Danny and Sandy both smiled at her comment. "For sure," Sandy nodded. I hoped this meant she was open to religious faith.

When Ginna got home from work that evening, we gathered for a basic dinner of meatloaf and baked potatoes from the garden. By the end of the meal, Ginna and Sandy were talking about all sorts of girl things, like hair styles, make-up, and what the new clothing fashions were.

"I like living in the country," my daughter was saying. "Out here people don't worry as much about the latest thing. We can dress in what we like."

"And what feels comfortable," Sandy added. "Give me a good pair of blue-jeans and a plaid flannel shirt, and I'm set."

I smiled across the table at Danny. He'd chosen wisely, it appeared.

Annie volunteered to help with dishes so the others could move to the living room and talk more. I was pleased with her being so observant of the situation.

Once the dishes were done, I realized that sleeping arrangements were going to be tricky. Our house had only three small bedrooms—counting the attic—each already occupied. Annie was using Danny's attic room while he was away at college.

"So how are we going to decide who sleeps where?" I asked.

"I can go back to my mom's room," piped up Annie. "Then Danny can have his old room back."

My son shook his head. "I don't think that solves one problem."

"What's that?" asked Annie, in her six-year-old innocence.

Her mother came to the rescue. "Danny and Sandy can't sleep in the same bed until they're married, Annie."

"Oh. When are they going to get married?"

We all broke into laughter. Danny patted her blonde head,

saying, "We haven't decided yet, Annie. I'll let you know when we do, though."

Sandy was blushing, and I wondered how much significance to put on his remark. At least he wasn't going to sleep with her under our roof.

"I have an idea, though," he went on. "Would it be okay if Sandy slept in your room, Annie? I'll just make my bed down here on the couch."

"Sure!" Annie jumped up, ready to haul Sandy up the attic stairs right then.

"Hang on," I said. "I made us gingerbread for dessert tonight. Let's have that first. Then you can show Sandy your room."

Sandy was holding Danny's hand. Looking up, she said, "How did you know gingerbread was my absolute favorite?"

"Just lucky, I guess." I smiled into the girl's bright blue eyes.

It was indeed lucky, I thought, as I got out some paper plates I'd found at the Dollar Store. Decorated with green holly leaves and red berries, they'd been a splurge, and now they helped make this evening more festive.

"Why don't we move to the couch?" I suggested. "Then we can enjoy the Christmas tree."

"You don't mind if we eat in there?" asked Sandy.

"Of course not. We're not that formal here. Besides, the kitchen and living room are just one big room."

By the time I'd dished up the gingerbread and topped each piece with whipped cream, Danny had turned on the tree's lights. Our casual conversation continued while we ate and admired the tree.

"Did you cut this tree in the mountains?" Danny asked.

I cut a quick glance at Ginna. *Perhaps he's wondering if Dave is still in my life*, I thought.

"No, I couldn't handle tromping through the woods. We just went to one of those tree yards in Greeley."

"How *are* you feeling, Mom?" Now I heard the hesitation in his voice.

"I'm better than I've been in a long time," I smiled. Looking at Sandy, I couldn't tell if he'd told her about the cancer and decided not to mention it unless he did. *After all, I'm in remission now. There's no need to bring it up.*

As soon as Danny and Sandy came back from his car with their bags, Annie grabbed Sandy's hand and pulled her to the stairs. "Wait till you see my room," she gushed. "You'll love it. I even have a purple bedspread."

"Purple is my favorite color," Sandy grinned as she followed our enthusiastic little girl.

"She fits right in already," I murmured to my son, once the two girls were out of sight in the attic room.

"I knew she would," he nodded. "She grew up on a farm, so she's used to country life."

"And simple things. That's a great help in a fractured family like ours."

"Oh, Mom, our family isn't broken. It's different, but I'm getting used to it. I'm glad that you're well again." He looked at the floor, and I wondered if he was testing, trying to find out if I was truly cured.

"Yes, the doctor says I'm their poster child for the new treatment," I smiled into his eyes. Then I couldn't resist doing a bit of testing of my own. "It looks like this relationship of yours is getting serious."

"I do think she's the one, Mom. I don't want anything more than to marry her. I'm not sure I can wait two more years until I graduate."

"Have you given her a ring yet?"

"You know I can't afford one."

"Well, all I can say is try to get a good start financially. That means finishing college. Part of your dad's and my problem was marrying too young." In the back of my mind, I wondered if I should tell him the truth about his dad, but I still couldn't bear to–afraid it would devastate my son or cement another brick in the wall between us. I couldn't risk that.

"Mom, you don't need to lecture me. I'm an adult."

"Okay, okay." Where had my former son gone—replaced by this touchy young man?

He stared over my shoulder, avoiding my eyes. "I don't see you as an expert on marriage."

"That's a low blow," I retorted. "Look, I like Sandy, and I know you have a good heart and mind. I'm sorry. It's just that I love you and want the best for you. I can't stop being a mom."

He shrugged and looked down at the worn brown carpet on our floor. "Okay, I'm sorry, too. Just don't worry. We'll be all right."

There were so many things I wanted to say to him, but I could see he wasn't ready to hear them. Instead I turned and went to the linen closet in our only bathroom, getting out sheets and blankets for his bed on the couch.

***

We had just enough snow that Christmas to build snowmen in the yard. Ginna and Annie convinced Danny and Sandy to build snow forts, which led to a snowball fight. I watched them from the windows because the cold was too hard on me. Ever since the end of chemo, my chest ached often, and I was short of breath. I reminded myself to ask Doctor Jensen about this next time I saw her.

Early January of 2015 brought an Alberta Clipper, one of those roaring blizzards that swept straight down the plains from the prairie provinces of Canada. I was thankful Danny and Sandy were already back in Greeley when it hit. School was cancelled, and Ginna couldn't get to work, for the roads were enveloped in whiteouts. Drifts of packed snow piled higher and higher, especially through roadcuts, where the snow filled in between the high banks on either side of the road.

When the wind stopped, and the clouds began to break, a world of snow and ice castles revealed itself through our front window. Ginna finally let a restless Annie go out to play in the snowdrifts.

"Stay close to the house," she warned. "If the wind comes back, you might get lost out there. I've heard stories about it at work, how people couldn't find their front door, even when it was only a few feet away. Once it almost happened to Danny and me."

"I'll be careful, Mommy."

"You'd better," I added, sounding as stern as I could. In the meantime, I was trying to remember when this blizzard was that she'd experienced, but I couldn't.

Annie didn't stay out long, for even though the sun made it look warmer, the air was frigid. She was back in the house in a short time with cherry-red cheeks and nose.

"My snowballs are all falling apart," she said, as she pulled off her coat by the door.

"Yes, Annie. When it's this cold, it won't hold together. We call it dry snow."

"Yeah, Gramma, it felt like cold powder."

"That's why the skiers call it powder snow," Ginna nodded.

"Well, I like snowman snow better. This isn't as much fun." She had her boots off by then, and was rubbing her cold hands. "Can I have some hot cocoa?"

"Of course you *may*," I grinned.

"Why do you always correct our grammar and manners, Mom?"

"Well, I guess because my mother did," I shrugged. "Maybe it doesn't matter that much, but for some reason she thought so. I think she wanted to sound like she was educated, and not a poor girl from the Texas backcountry."

"Well, that's okay, I suppose," said Ginna.

"It was more of a big deal back then, too."

"Mom, do you ever miss Texas?"

This question took me by surprise. "Well, maybe when we're having really cold weather here—like today. What about you?"

"I think of the friends I left back there that I've lost touch with, wondering sometimes where they are now. But there's no way to find out. I've heard it said, 'You can't go home again.'"

"Yeah, I think that's a quote from a book by Thomas Wolfe."

I began mixing cocoa powder with hot water from the teakettle, adding tap water to Annie's to be sure it was cool enough for her to drink.

"I wonder sometimes about friends I lost, too." I set the mugs on the table. "But ever since the cancer scare, I just try to appreciate every day as it comes. Each day is a gift to me now."

My daughter nodded and sipped her cocoa. "That's a good reminder, for sure. I'll try to do that, too. Just enjoy each day I have with you and Annie."

There was a wistful tone in her voice that touched me. Was she thinking about Annie's father, even after all this time? She'd still never said any more about him, or what had actually happened. But I knew there was no point in asking her more questions. Either she didn't know, or she didn't want to remember.

CHAPTER 21
Stronger Winds

The first blizzard of 2015 was past, but more of them kept coming. Ginna and I had cabin fever, feeling cut off from the outside world. Even Annie, usually happy as long as she had a book to read, was restless.

After the winds stopped, the drifts kept some of the backroads treacherous. School buses had trouble completing their routes. So many snow days piled up that Annie's school would probably go well into June to make up. When the first day of spring came at last, we were all so glad for rain instead of snow that we ran outside to play in the puddles.

I hadn't heard much from Danny through these months, and wondered why. All I could do was assume he was getting to classes at UNC when they weren't cancelled by the storms. Whenever I tried to call, all I got was his voicemail. If I left a message, he never called back.

By the tenth of April, the country roads were passable again. The very next Saturday, Danny and Sandy pulled into our driveway.

"Hi, Mom," he called as they climbed the old wooden porch steps.

I gave them both hugs and led them to the kitchen table, pouring some of the coffee I'd made just a short while before. "I'm so glad to see you two safe and sound. Why didn't you call me?"

"Sorry, Mom. Some days our phones were out because of damage to the cell towers. And we've been really busy."

"With school?"

He looked down for a moment before he answered. "Yes, that, and other things." He glanced aside at Sandy, and I felt a sudden tightness in my chest. "We got married and found a small house to rent in Eaton."

I plopped down on a kitchen chair, speechless.

When I didn't say anything, he hurried on. "Don't worry, we're not pregnant yet. We just decided we couldn't wait, especially with such a hard winter. All the storms made us feel like you never know what can happen, and we didn't want to take the chance of putting things off."

"I guess I can agree with that." I took a deep breath. Why did my chest hurt so much? "Do her parents know?"

"Yes, and I'm still going to finish my degree, so don't be angry, please." He reached over and took his wife's hand. "There didn't seem to be any point in making a big deal. Sandy's family couldn't come with all the blizzards, and you guys were snowed in a lot. So we just went to the Justice of the Peace."

In spite of my attempts, tears were welling in my eyes. No wedding to celebrate with my son, and Ginna didn't seem to have any interest in marriage, either. In a little rural town like Deer Path, there wasn't much chance to meet any prospects, even for myself. I'd put thoughts of remarrying aside long ago, after Dave moved away, but now the cancer diagnosis took it off my list permanently. How could I burden someone else with the possibility of recurring cancer?

Danny rose from his chair and gave me a firm hug. "Mom, please don't be sad. We're going to be fine."

I melted into his embrace, thankful that at least he'd opened up a bit more.

A couple of weeks later, Ginna drove Annie and me to Eaton to see Danny and Sandy's rental house. All the way, I kept trying to wrap my head around everything. My son was married, and barely twenty-one. Of course, I'd married even younger than that, but I shut these thoughts down before I dwelt on what had happened to my marriage.

While we drove, Ginna began to talk about Danny. "I know things have been tense between you two sometimes, Mom. Maybe you don't realize how hard the divorce was on him. After all, he's been the only male in a house full of females."

"You know, I have thought of that. I had to fill both roles, mother and father. But I don't think I did it very well."

"You did your best, which is all anyone can expect. Still, Danny has told me he misses having a male role-model."

"I know the emptiness your dad left. It's too bad he just cut us off."

"Yeah, now I understand why you felt the need for a man."

"Let's not go there right now, Ginna." I glanced toward the back seat where Annie was gazing out the window.

We rode in silence the rest of the way.

Danny and Sandy's house was a small brick one near downtown. Eaton wasn't as big as Greeley, but more of a town than Deer Path.

As Danny and Sandy led us through their front door, I noted the spartan furniture, a sagging couch and one easy chair.

"This place came furnished," he said, noticing my look. "Someday we'll be able to afford better furniture."

"Hey, this is fine," said Ginna.

"Yeah!" Annie plopped herself on the gray-green couch. "This is comfy." The remains of its tufted upholstery revealed its 1950s origins.

I smiled, too. "Well, it fits our style. You know our furniture is pretty basic."

Ginna and I joined Annie, while Sandy took the brown Naugahyde easy chair. Once we were all seated in this small living room, Danny grabbed a chair from the kitchen so he'd have a place to sit. They were also 1950s style, with metal legs. Green plastic-covered seats and backs were attached to the frame with silver bolts.

"This furniture is really retro," said Ginna.

"It works for now," Sandy smiled.

Just then a large brown and black striped cat ambled into the room.

"Wow, you have a kitty," cried Annie. She was delighted when the cat jumped onto the couch and began purring as she petted it. "Can we get a kitty, Mom?"

Ginna frowned. "I'm not home enough to take care of a cat."

"Cats are really independent, Sis," said Danny. "Once they're litter-box trained, they can be left for a couple of days even, as long as there's enough food and water."

"Okay, I'll think about it. But it's really up to Mom. It's her house we live in after all."

"Can we please get a cat, Gramma?"

While this conversation was going, I was focused on a sudden sharp pain in my upper back. I'd put off seeing Doctor Jensen too long, but the blizzards had been part of my excuse. Turning to Annie, I smiled, "We'll think about it. Okay?"

Annie kept stroking the cat. "What's her name, Uncle Danny?"

"It's a he," grinned Danny. "We call him Feier."

"You mean like a campfire?" Annie asked.

"No," he chuckled. "It's not spelled f-i-r-e. It's a German word I think, f-e-i-e-r. A friend of mine named his cat that, and I like to be reminded of him."

For some reason, Ginna rose from the couch at this and said, "Hey, Annie, let's go see what your uncle's yard looks like. I need some sunshine."

Danny nodded and rose to join them. "The back yard is fenced, so go on out the kitchen door. We even have a space where we'll be putting a vegetable garden."

"Was there something wrong?" asked Sandy.

I shook my head. "I don't know. Ginna still won't talk about how she got pregnant. I'm worried for her. What if she went through some deep trauma she can't deal with?"

"Still, she seems to be a good mother to Annie."

"I am grateful to have Ginna living with me. It would have been much harder to face the breast cancer alone."

Sandy nodded again but sadness washed over her face. Her voice dropped to a whisper. "Danny mentioned it, but I think it's hard for him to talk about. Are you cured now?"

"My oncologist says I'm in remission. No one knows how long that may last. It might be years, or just weeks."

Sandy rose and joined me on the couch, taking my hand. "We'll pray it's years."

CHAPTER 22
Down the Well

Just a week later, I went to see Doctor Jensen when she came to her Greeley office, thankful that I didn't have to go all the way to Denver. I was feeling weak, and all the traffic made that drive too stressful for me. After my appointment, I planned to stop by Eaton to pay a visit to Danny and Sandy, if they were home. I hadn't phoned them because all this was last-minute planning. The doctor's office had called just that morning, asking if I could come a week earlier than my original appointment.

After all the usual preliminaries, I waited in the exam room for longer than usual, getting nervous. Sitting in the uncomfortable wooden chair with sweaty hands, I kept tapping my feet on the carpeted floor. At last the doctor came in and asked how I'd been feeling. When I told her about the back pain and shortness of breath, concern came over her face.

"I'd better listen to you breathe," she said, putting her stethoscope to her ears and holding it to my back. "Take a deep breath for me." She shifted to the other side and repeated these directions. Then she moved to my chest. "Breathe normally, please."

Now there was definitely concern in her voice.

"Is there a problem?" I asked.

"Something doesn't sound right, Lauren. I think we're going to need a chest x-ray and a lung biopsy to find out more."

My heart sank. "Has the cancer moved there?"

She patted my shoulder. "Don't panic. We don't know anything for sure. It could just be a touch of bronchitis."

I nodded and tried to smile. "Okay."

"I'll need you to go to the cancer clinic in Fort Collins for more tests."

By the time I left the office, an appointment was scheduled for the following week. As I got into the car, numbness was setting into my mind. Part of me had dreaded this, and part of me was in denial. *This can't be happening. I thought the Lord had cured me of this cancer. But it may not be cancer. You still don't know for sure,* I tried to convince myself.

Now I was wishing I'd let Ginna drive me to this appointment, but I hadn't wanted to mess up her work schedule at the last minute. For a long time, all I could do was sit in the car, wiping at tears and trying to pray.

When I finally got myself collected, I discovered it was beginning to snow.

"Oh, thanks," I muttered to the windshield. "Just what I needed, a spring snowstorm."

I was still driving our ten-year-old Echo. Ginna had finally been able to afford a car of her own this year, a used all-wheel-drive Subaru Outback. At least she would do all right driving in this snow.

As I started out of the parking lot, the snow swirled thicker, running in thin white waves across the black asphalt. Even though Ginna's office was here in Greeley, I decided not to bother her. All I really wanted now was to get home and crawl into bed.

By the time I reached Eaton, the snow was sticking to the pavement and the road was getting icy. As I drove by Danny's rental, I was dismayed to see his car wasn't there. Tears were blurring my vision, so I pulled over in front of the little house anyway and killed the engine. Overcome, I rested my head on the steering wheel and took deep breaths to calm myself. At last, I reached for the ignition to restart the car.

Just then, there came a loud rapping on my window. Looking over my left shoulder, I saw Sandy, wearing a red hooded sweatshirt that was already plastered with snow. I opened my window about two inches.

"Lauren, is something wrong? Do you want to come in?"

Speechless, all I could do was nod, as I pulled the key out of the ignition and grabbed my purse. By the time we dashed through the frigid wind and stumbled the few yards to the house, I was panting for breath and shivering with cold.

"Here, let me help you," said Sandy, taking my coat and hanging it on a hook by the door. "What brought you out in this spring storm?"

"Doctor's appointment," I managed to gasp.

"Come sit by the woodstove." She guided me to a wooden rocking chair.

"Is this chair new?" I murmured, not remembering it from our first visit.

"Sort of. We found it at the Thrift Store in Greeley"

"It's nice."

"Would you like a cup of tea? All I have today is English Breakfast."

"That's my favorite."

"I'll have to heat the water on the stove. We don't have a microwave yet."

"That's okay."

Soon the teakettle whistled, and she poured steaming water over the teabags in each cup.

"This storm was a big surprise, wasn't it?" Sandy handed me warm a cup.

I nodded and sipped, still trying to gather myself. The warm liquid felt wonderful, gradually filling my body with comfort. This was the tea my mother had always liked.

"Danny's at a class," Sandy continued. "He won't be home for a couple of hours, I'm afraid. Why didn't you tell us you were coming?" Her voice was filled with concern.

I took a deep breath, trying to ignore the heaviness in my chest. "It was supposed to be next week, but Doctor Jensen had a cancellation. They called this morning, so it was last-minute."

"Is Doctor Jensen your regular doctor?"

"She's my oncologist."

"Oh, is everything all right?"

Such a simple question, but I burst into tears. For a long time, all I could do was shake my head.

"I don't know yet. They want to do an x-ray and lung biopsy next week."

Sandy moved one of the green kitchen chairs close to me and took my hand. "We'll pray they don't find any cancer." Before I could say another word, she began to pray aloud:

"Dear Lord, you know the plans you have for each of us, plans to give us hope and a future. I pray that you will give Lauren peace of mind in this frightening time. Help her and all of her family to trust and lean on you. We pray there is no returning cancer, but if there is, we ask for healing, and for wisdom for the doctors who serve Lauren. Amen."

"Amen," I sighed. Tears were still flooding my eyes, and Sandy brought a napkin from the table so I could wipe them.

"Ginna shared that Bible verse with me once, the one about God knowing the plans he has for us."

"It's in the book of Jeremiah, but I can't remember the chapter and verse."

"That's okay, Sandy. God knows. Thank you for praying with me. I'm blessed to have you for a daughter."

She hugged me, and more comfort flowed into my body. We remained seated there a long time, holding each other's hands.

"Goodness, look at the time," Sandy said, turning to the clock on their kitchen wall. "I need to start dinner. Won't you stay?"

"I don't want to be a bother."

"You're no bother. If this snow doesn't let up by dark, you can even stay the night. I know Danny will insist. There's a bed in our spare bedroom."

"But I need to get home for Annie."

"Why don't you call or text Ginna?"

"Okay. Maybe she can get off early, with this weather. We did give Annie a house key for emergencies."

"From what I've seen of your granddaughter, she's pretty self-reliant."

"True."

By this time, I had the phone out of my purse and speed dialed Ginna. Relief washed over me when she answered.

"Are you okay, Mom?" Ginna heard the quaver in my voice.

"Yes, I'm fine. My appointment with Doctor Jensen was moved up to today."

"Are you there now? I can pick you up. I hope you're not driving in this storm."

"I'm at Danny and Sandy's house."

"Mom, you just stay there. Wait until tomorrow to see if the weather clears. The roads will be even worse after dark."

"But what about Annie, when she gets off the school bus?"

"I'm sure my boss will let me leave here early when I explain the circumstances."

"I don't want you to jeopardize your job for me."

"No, Mom. It will be fine. Please stay with Danny and don't worry. We'll work it out."

"Okay, Honey." As I signed off, I realized I hadn't said anything about the biopsy next week. I wasn't ready to break the news to her.

Sandy was already getting a casserole into the oven.

"Wow, that was fast."

"Oh, it's my lazy-day chicken and rice. All I have to do is put rice and chicken breasts into the dish and pour a can of soup over it all. Danny likes it with cheese on top. I hope you do."

"Anything I don't have to cook is fine with me." I managed a smile. "All you children have been so good to me. I'm a blessed mother."

***

Danny arrived as the casserole was coming out of the oven. Sandy had made a tossed salad while it was cooking.

"Mmm, smells good," he said as he came in the door. He turned to me, where I sat in the rocking chair. "Mom, what are you doing here? I saw your car. Is everything all right?"

"I had a last-minute doctor appointment," I began.

"I insisted she stay until after the storm lets up," added Sandy.

She gave me a smile, and I was thankful she avoided talking about the oncologist right then.

"Dinner's ready, if you are," she smiled at her husband.

"Famished." He hung his coat on the hook next to mine.

As we ate, I thought about what to tell him, wondering if Sandy would say something first.

Once the dishes were cleared, Sandy put them in the sink and ran hot soapy water over them. "I'm sorry, we don't usually do dessert," she was saying. "Except for special occasions."

"Oh, that's no problem." I smiled. "I need to watch my sweets anyway."

Sandy glanced from me to Danny, then turned to washing the dishes. I knew this was my cue.

"I saw Doctor Jensen today."

"Is that the oncologist?"

I nodded to him.

"What did she say, Mom?"

"Well, she listened to me breathe, and ordered a lung biopsy for next week."

"In Greeley?"

"No, in Fort Collins."

"I don't want you to drive that far alone," he said. "Besides, you may not be allowed to drive afterwards, you know."

"But I don't want you missing classes for me, son."

"When is this appointment?"

"Next Tuesday at ten AM."

"Hmm. I have a lecture then, but I can probably miss it."

"No, Danny. Maybe Ginna can take me."

"Then she'll have to take off work, and there's the problem of who can meet Annie's school bus," he said.

"I know. Ginna had to get off early today for that because I couldn't be there in time."

"Yeah, Sis texted me. She said to be sure you didn't try to drive home alone tonight."

"So my children are parenting me," I laughed.

"Just returning the favor," he patted my hand where it rested on the table.

"I have an idea, Danny," Sandy said from the kitchen sink. "I could take her to Fort Collins, if you can get by without the car for one day."

"I suppose that would work. If you dropped me off in Greeley on your way, I could just hang out on campus all day. There's research I need to do in the library, anyway."

"But what if I end up having to stay overnight?" I murmured.

"Ginna and I will work out something, Mom. We're old enough to take care of ourselves."

I squeezed his hand that was still holding mine. "I know you are. I'm lucky—and thankful."

CHAPTER 23
Walking Through the Valley

It was a good thing Sandy volunteered to take me to the Fort Collins appointment, because the Friday before, I received directions stating I might be under anesthesia for the biopsy, and to plan for someone to drive me home. Unlike Danny, who had classes and an on-campus part-time job, Sandy worked only weekends as a waitress at a small restaurant in Eaton. I hesitated to ask what her plans were—if they included continuing college now that they were married.

"Why don't I drive as far as your house to save time?" I asked as we discussed plans on the phone.

"It's easier for me to come by and pick you up, since you're north of Greeley," said Sandy. "That's more on my way to Fort Collins from Eaton. I have to take Danny to Greeley at about seven AM, too. You'd have to come too early if you drove here."

At last, I decided to stop planning, and let the kids take care of me for a change. It was an awkward feeling, after being the mom for so many years.

When Sandy pulled into the driveway at eight that Tuesday morning, they'd organized everything. Ginna was going to bring Danny home from Greeley in mid-afternoon, then head home so she'd be back at the house in time to meet Annie's school bus.

"All I have to concentrate on is you, Lauren," Sandy smiled.

As she drove north and then west toward Fort Collins, the

sun was shining over our right shoulders and then behind us. The grass of the plains was greening-up with that fresh color of spring. Some snowdrifts were still nestled in sheltered gullies and on north-facing slopes.

"I love when spring comes. It's the most beautiful time on the prairies," I said.

"It is great to see the colors after the drabness of winter," Sandy nodded. "But I also like fall when the rolling valleys are golden with ripe wheat and corn."

"Yes, I can see that the fields would be nicer east of here."

"I'm just a Kansas farmgirl. I miss the big grain fields. They look richer than these dry high plains. This land was part of the Great Dust Bowl of the 1930s, wasn't it?"

"I think so, Sandy. Maybe that's why it seems more barren than Kansas. More of the topsoil here blew away. It was all before I was born. Those must have been really hard times for a lot of people."

Sandy nodded. "My grandparents would tell stories about it sometimes, but I don't think they liked to talk about it much."

In silence, we watched the scenery continue to slide by.

"I'm hoping that when Danny finishes his agribusiness degree, I can go back to school. We can't afford to pay tuition for both of us right now."

I was glad Sandy had brought this up without prompting from me.

"Has Danny said what he hopes to do when he graduates?" I'd hesitated to ask this, but pressed on anyway. It seemed easier to talk to my daughter-in-law than to my son these days. He still got defensive whenever I asked about his plans.

"He hopes to get a job managing a farm supply store or working for a farm loan company. I'm interested in environmental science and range management. I'd like to work with farmers and ranchers to improve their yields and their care for the land. Colorado State in Fort Collins has the best program, so we're hoping we'll find work and a house close by, so I can commute there."

"Well, those both sound like good jobs to keep you nearby in Colorado."

"That's what we hope, too."

***

After this pleasant drive, I was not prepared for the ordeal that followed. Three hours after we arrived at the Fort Collins Hospital Cancer Center, I was lying in a hospital bed, still groggy and confused. It brought back memories of when I'd wakened in the recovery room after my mastectomy. Not something I wanted to be reminded of.

No one was in sight until a young man came to take my blood pressure. "How are you feeling?"

"Sore," I said. As soon as I shifted just a little, pain shot through my right side, just below my ribcage. "What happened?"

"They did a lung biopsy. Don't you remember?"

"Only sort of. When will I know the results? Can I see my daughter-in-law?"

"Is she waiting for you?"

"Yes."

"What's her name?"

"Sandy Parker."

"I'll have someone call her to come in," he smiled.

Long minutes passed until I finally saw Sandy's familiar face and long red hair. She pulled a wooden chair up to the side of the bed and took my hand. I relaxed when she joined me, smiling into her bright blue eyes.

"Are you doing all right, Lauren?"

"I'm sore. I wish they'd give me something for the pain."

"The nurse told me they already did."

"Oh. I hope a doctor comes soon to tell me what's up."

I must have dozed off, because the next time I opened my eyes, Sandy was talking to a man in a white coat.

"I'm awake, doctor," I murmured. "Am I going to die?"

Sandy looked shocked when I said this, but he didn't. This did not bode well.

"You're not going to die immediately," he said. "Of course, we all die eventually, you know."

"Okay." I didn't need these word games. "What did they find?"

"Your x-ray showed quite a few spots in your lungs. We won't have pathology results for a few days, but some of your tissue does appear to be compromised."

"Compromised by cancer?"

"We can't say that definitively."

"But you suspect, don't you?"

"We have to wait for pathology's report."

Sandy squeezed my hand, her lips moving, probably in a prayer. I was thankful for her presence.

A week later, I was back in Doctor Jensen's office in Greeley. Ginna had insisted on coming with me this time, and going into the exam room, too. There was no arguing with her, and despite myself, I was thankful for the emotional support.

When Doctor Jensen entered, there was no doubt about the look on her face. "I'm sorry, Lauren," she began. "They've found spots of cancer throughout both lungs. It must be an aggressive carcinoma to have spread this much in such a short time."

"What can you do about it?" Ginna demanded.

"It appears to be inoperable." The doctor shook her head and looked toward me. "I don't recommend a lung transplant in your condition, either."

"I couldn't afford that anyway," I murmured.

"Well, if this cancer is as aggressive as I think, you wouldn't be able to survive the wait for a suitable donor."

"Isn't there some kind of chemo or radiation you can do?" asked Ginna.

"It would have to be radiation," said Doctor Jensen. "And strong. It might help, or it might not."

"I wonder if it's worth it," I sighed.

Ginna grabbed my hand. "No, Mom. Don't say that. Anything is worth a try, if it helps you live longer."

Seeing the look in her eyes, I nodded. "You're right. I'm not ready to say my goodbyes to you children yet. There are things I have to get settled. For one thing, I need to find a lawyer and write a will. I just never expected to need one this early in my life."

"Life is never a certainty," Doctor Jensen murmured.

"No, it's not. I guess you see that more often than most of us."

She patted my shoulder. "Yes, unfortunately, I do see it much too frequently."

***

On the drive home, Ginna was very quiet. I couldn't think of anything to say, either. What can you say when you know your days are numbered? At last, though, I couldn't take the silence any longer.

"I don't want you to tell Annie or Danny. I need to think about how to do it myself."

"I understand. I don't know what I'd say anyway."

I heard tears in her voice, though there were none on her cheeks.

"What is there to say? I need to get right with God first."

"You know Jesus is your savior, Mom. That's all it takes."

"I've always believed that, Ginna. But when you're looking down that valley of the shadow of death, it's different."

"Even though I walk through the dark valley of death, I will fear no evil. For you are with me—"

"Yes, Psalm twenty-three. I've known that since I was a child. But children have no concept of what that word death means, do they?"

"Oh, I don't know. When Dad left us, I felt like something inside me died, even though I was only twelve."

"Of course I did, too. For me it was the death of all my dreams, almost my everything."

"You still had Danny and me."

"That's what kept me going. I couldn't let myself just die and leave you two alone."

"You mean you thought of suicide?"

"Once or twice." I was surprised to hear myself admitting this to her. "When Dave came along, I thought he was heaven-sent. He gave me joy and love again. I mattered to another man."

"But Mom—"

"Don't say it. I know it was wrong, but it was all I had for a while."

"You know, I did like him in the end."

"He was a likable person. There was something about him, but I can't find the right words for it."

"I noticed it, too," sighed Ginna. "You could tell he was trying to be kind and sincere."

"You know the last time I saw him was at that Communications Conference in Spokane, when we were asked to talk about our special project on the HTGR. That was after he transferred to Sheboygan, Wisconsin."

"I remember when you went. I was afraid you'd start the affair again."

"Well, by then I knew I shouldn't, Honey, but I was really tempted. He respected my choices, though. The last thing I told him the day he flew out of Spokane was I hoped he'd accept Jesus as his savior."

"Really? What did he say?"

"It was heart-breaking. He said he didn't feel the need for a savior."

"Oh."

"Then I told him I hoped someday, he *would* feel the need, and that when he did he'd remember what I said."

"I wonder if that ever happened."

"There's no way to know now. I'll never hear from him again, but I told him I hoped to see him in heaven when I got there."

"Gosh, Mom. You really gave a bold witness."

"I don't know if it did any good, but at least I tried."

We settled into silence again for several miles. As we were making the turn onto the cutoff to Deer Path, I heard her sigh It sounded like she murmured something to herself.

"What did you say, Honey?"

"Nothing, Mom. Except I just want you to know how much I love and respect you."

"I'm nowhere near perfect. I've made a lot of huge mistakes."

"But God has used you. And you're still with us right now. So He's not finished with you yet."

"No, I suppose He isn't, is He?"

CHAPTER 24
Learning to Flow

I tried that stronger radiation therapy for six weeks, but it left me weak and exhausted. When Ginna was home in the evenings, her presence helped—along with Annie's. But soon the long shuttle ride to Fort Collins became too much for me, though it was only twice a week and not as far as Denver. Then even the evenings at home became difficult.

One night when Ginna got home, I was lying on the couch, wrapped in two blankets to ward off the chills. It wasn't working.

"Mom, you look so weary." She came to sit in the chair opposite me.

"I am, Honey. I don't think I can go on like this. Poor Annie gets home and has to do everything for herself. I'm no help at all. She reads to me, but I usually fall asleep. When I wake, she's gone upstairs to her room."

"It's all right, Mom. I know she understands."

"But I want so much to be here for her. What's the point of my being here if all I am is a burden to you?"

"I don't mind, really."

"You have to get up so early and drag Annie out of bed to take me to the shuttle. This is just too much."

Ginna brushed at her cheek. Was that a tear? "You're worth any extra effort we make, Mom."

"What kind of life can I give you?"

"Look, why don't we go see Doctor Jensen and talk about this? Maybe there's another treatment that won't be as tough on you."

"All right. I'll go, if you'll come with me."

"Of course I will."

A week later, we were talking with Doctor Jensen in her Greeley office, one morning when Annie was at school. Ginna was holding my hand.

"I can't go on with this treatment, doctor. It's like I'm only half-alive."

She listened, then turned to my daughter. "What do you think?"

"Me? Well, I can't speak for my mom. For myself, I don't want to lose her. But if it's inevitable—"

Her voice broke and she grabbed for a tissue.

"I'm nothing but a burden to my children now," I sighed. "I don't want them wasting their energies on my waning life."

"It sounds like you could use some in-home care."

"How does that work?"

"Well, if you decide to terminate your treatment, we'll have to assess you every week, to see how much you are declining. If you get to the point where I determine you aren't likely to survive another six months, I can put you on Hospice Care."

"I've heard of that," Ginna interrupted. "Isn't it for the very end of life?"

"In many cases, yes," the doctor nodded. "But some patients go through two or three six-month periods before the end."

"The end," I murmured. "There are days when I wish this struggle would end."

"Mom, please don't say that!"

"I'm sorry, Ginna" said Doctor Jensen. "I know this is difficult for both of you. But this is your mother's decision as long she's mentally capable."

My daughter's shoulders were shaking in silent sobs. I reached over and took her hand. "Please. It's not as though I'm going to commit suicide. I just want to see what other options I have besides more of this radiation. I want to find a way—if there is one—to have some quality in the last days, or months, of my life."

"Yes, that's what Hospice is meant for," said the doctor. "There is support for the family, too. If this is what your mother wants, it will help to take some of the burden off you, Ginna."

"Can we take some time to think about this and talk it over?" Ginna asked.

"Of course you can. I'm not here to force you into anything. Should we make another appointment, say for this time next week?"

"Yes," Ginna nodded.

The drive home that day was mostly silent. I didn't know what to say, and evidently Ginna didn't want to talk either. We neared Deer Path before my daughter spoke.

"You have to talk to Danny about this hospice idea."

"Yes, I know. But I'm not sure Annie will understand."

"Let's wait and see how this goes. Didn't the doctor say they would monitor you weekly to see if you declined?"

"I believe she did."

***

I didn't tell Ginna right away, but some of my energy began to come back after I'd been off the radiation for a couple of weeks. Doctor Jensen monitored me each week, either personally or through one of her physician assistants. Most of these appointments were able to take place over the phone or via the Internet, so we didn't have to drive to Greeley or Denver every week.

After the first month, the doctor told us, "I'm pleasantly surprised with how you're doing, Lauren. I see a bit more color in your cheeks, and your breathing is good. It appears you were correct to drop the radiation."

"Maybe you'll turn into a walking miracle, Mom," said Ginna.

"Only God knows. But I'll trust Him for whatever He plans."

"I'll try to do the same," nodded my daughter.

As spring moved into summer that year, I gained enough strength to meet with a lawyer in Greeley and prepare my will. "I want to leave my children with something," I told him. "Not just a pile of medical bills."

"We'll do the best we can. It helps that you own a house."

"Yes, it was lucky I decided to purchase it a few years ago, shortly before my granddaughter was born. Even though I wasn't sick then, I wanted my daughter to have a place to live if something ever happened to me. The landlord wanted to sell it, and gave a reasonable price, so I jumped at the chance. Interests rates were low enough then, and the monthly payment was about the same as my rent. Since it was a contract with him, it's almost paid off."

"A very fortunate move."

"I wish I could give my son something, though."

"Are there any other assets you could leave your son?"

"Not really. All I have is my house."

"Perhaps the best thing is to leave the house to both your children, if you think they get along well enough to deal with that."

I pondered this for a moment before nodding. "Yes, I think so. They've always been close, especially since my husband left us."

"There's no child support from him?"

"He rarely followed through on that. Now both my children are over twenty-one, so it's all water under the bridge."

"You don't want to try suing him? That is a possibility."

"No. It's better to let sleeping dogs lie."

He smiled. "You are a wealth of proverbs, Lauren."

"My mother was."

"Do your children have grandparents?"

"No, my parents died while I was a teenager. I haven't heard from their paternal grandparents in years and don't even know if they're still living."

After this meeting, he drew up a basic will stating that I left all my assets to my children, to be divided equally between them, with a Pay On Death Clause, which prevented any possible complications with probate. He also drew up a Power of Attorney giving Ginna the right to speak for me, if I became unable. Once these documents were signed and witnessed by his office staff, I felt like another burden had been lifted from me.

On the way home that day, a whim hit me, and I drove to the Humane Society. There I selected a brown-striped kitten to bring home to Annie.

Not long after this, though, weakness began to creep into me again. I'd held on just long enough to get everything taken care of. I tried to keep this from Ginna as long as I could.

Summer days brought a warmth which was welcome. I spent as much time as I could in a chair on the front porch. Most days, I watched Annie playing on the tire swing we'd hung from a big cottonwood tree in the yard. Annie loved to swing and could do it for hours.

When Annie finally tired, she'd come sit on the porch with me and we'd sip lemonade she made from those powders you mix with water. Many times we chuckled at the antics her kitten got into. His name was Tigger, and he climbed and bounced around much like his namesake in the *Winnie the Pooh* stories. Annie would tell about the books she was reading, and sometimes made up stories of her own about dragons and gallant knights.

One day, my granddaughter said something that floored me, though. "Gramma, how much longer do you think you'll live?"

"Oh, Annie, nobody knows the answer to a question like that. Only God does."

"But Gramma, I know your cancer has gotten worse. I can tell by how Mommy looks at you."

I'd thought we were doing a better job of keeping things from her, but it appeared Annie was too perceptive.

"I hope I get to see you start school in the fall, sweetie. Some days I get very tired. But other days, like today, I feel pretty good. Having you to talk to helps me a lot."

"When I tell stories?"

"Especially then," I smiled. "And when the sun is shining."

Annie looked toward the sky, where some fluffy white clouds were gliding above the plains. "I hope the sun shines every day this summer, Gramma."

"Well, we do need rain sometimes, too. Otherwise the crops will wilt, and so will our garden. Life can't be sunny all the time."

She pulled at the grass by her feet. "I suppose so. Is that why life can't always be happy? Is that why people have to die?"

"My, those are deep thoughts for a girl not even in second grade yet."

I searched for more words. What would my own mother have said about this all those years ago? "Annie, God loves us all, and if we trust Him, He'll take us to be with Him in heaven when we die. I'll be there a long time before you, I think. But I'll be waiting right at the gates, and I'll see you again in that place, even though I have to die and leave you here for now."

I saw her swipe at a single tear. "Let's sing a song, Gramma. I want to think about God loving us, instead of talking about dying."

"Come here, sweetie." I drew her into the chair and held her close. "What should we sing?"

"What about *Jesus Loves Me*, okay?"

So we sang to the sunshine, the clouds, the birds in the trees, and the grass in the fields. Both of us holding back tears.

CHAPTER 25
Lifted Up

Summer was edging into fall, and Annie was talking about back-to-school shopping–new crayons and pencils, new shoes and clothes. It was a joy to anticipate with her. I gathered my strength and went with my daughter and granddaughter to shop in Greeley.

The next morning, though, I was too weak to get out of bed.

Looks like you overdid it, I said to myself.

Since Ginna was already at work, I called for Annie, who came bouncing in, but her expression fell when she saw me.

"Gramma, you look sick," she cried.

"It's all right, Honey. I'm just tired from the shopping trip yesterday. Do you think you could bring me some orange juice and a piece of toast? I feel like breakfast in bed today."

"Sure," she bounded out of the room.

I was thankful I'd managed not to worry her, but there was nothing else I could do. My body was refusing to move.

Breakfast left my stomach upset, and I prayed I wouldn't vomit. After lying on my back for about an hour, I called for my granddaughter.

"Annie, could you find some extra pillows, so I can get propped up?"

Again, she dashed to help, bringing two pillows from her mom's room.

Getting to a sitting position was a little easier with Annie's help. The next issue would be getting myself to the toilet.

I waited as long as I could, knowing I wouldn't be strong enough for this task. At last, I called Annie.

"Could you please bring me my phone?"

When she returned, I noticed more worry in her eyes.

"It's all right, Annie. I just need to talk to my friend Grace. You go read a book, okay?"

"Can I go outside to play now?"

"Yes, go ahead." I hoped Grace could come over, so I wouldn't be stuck without any help. And I didn't want to upset Annie by asking her to stay with me.

Relief filled me when Grace answered the call. She had been a great support through this long cancer ordeal, often bringing a meal when Ginna had to work late, and all of us were too tired to cook.

"Lauren, are you all right? You don't sound good."

"I'm not doing well today. Do you think you could come over and help me? Ginna's at work, and I don't want to worry Annie."

"Of course, I'll be right there."

Grace lived only a mile up the road, so she was at the door in a matter of minutes.

Annie followed her in, with a worried look on her face. I did my best to smile and wave at them. "Oh, Grace, it's so good to see you. I've been wanting to tell you about this book I just finished. Annie, you can go back outside and play." Annie gave me a peck on the cheek and dashed out the door.

"Now tell me the truth," said Grace, seating herself on a chair next to the bed.

"I went shopping in Greeley yesterday with Ginna and

Annie. I wanted to be part of their back-to-school excitement, but now I feel so weak I can barely move."

"What can I do first?"

"I need the toilet desperately."

"Okay." Before another word was said, Grace was holding me under my arms, giving support so I could get out of bed.

Once we'd been to the toilet and back, I was even more exhausted. "I've never felt so wiped out. Even when I was on chemo."

Grace held my hand, now that I was settled back on my pile of pillows. "I think it's time to call your doctor," she murmured.

"Yes, I suppose so."

I called Doctor Jensen's office, but had to leave a voice mail, hoping I'd get a call back before too much time went by.

While Grace was sitting beside my bed, she began humming some of our favorite hymns, like *Amazing Grace*. Listening to the sound, I began to relax. I must have fallen asleep, for the next thing I knew my phone was ringing, and I fumbled to answer it.

"Lauren, this is Doctor Jensen. Is there a problem?"

"Thanks so much for calling me back. I think it may be time for Hospice to come in."

"What's going on?"

"I'm so weak, I can hardly move. In fact I had to call my neighbor to help me to the toilet. It's too much for my granddaughter to handle alone. Besides, she starts school next week, and no one will be here with me."

"It does sound like time for you to have some help. You're sure about going on Hospice?"

"Yes, I can tell I'm getting near the end, doctor."

I glanced at Grace as I said this and saw my friend's cheeks shining with tears.

"I think you're probably right, Lauren. Frankly, you've lasted longer than I thought you would."

"Thank you for being up-front with me."

"Some things we just have to face. I'll get the paperwork started today."

"I'm ready, you know," I murmured. "It's been a hard life, but a good one. And where I'm going will be even better."

Both Grace and I were weeping when I signed off the call. Without any words, she embraced me, holding me in her arms for a long time.

I must have fallen asleep again. The next thing I knew, Ginna was home.

"Ginna," I said in surprise, when I saw her at the bedroom door. "You didn't have to come home early."

"I'm not early, Mom. You must have slept the afternoon away. Are you okay?"

I tried to nod, but even this didn't work for me.

Then Ginna saw Grace seated beside me. "Have you been here long, Grace?"

"Not really. Just this afternoon." I knew my friend was stretching the truth, but made no comment.

Once Ginna was on the other side of the bed, I grasped my daughter's hand. "I called the doctor to start Hospice care. A visiting nurse will be coming tomorrow."

"Mom, no—" Her eyes grew red and tears filled them. "You're just tired from yesterday."

"No, Honey, I can tell. I think Doctor Jensen knew I'd be calling soon. She already had everything in the works, I'm sure. Otherwise the nurse wouldn't be coming tomorrow already."

By now Ginna was sobbing and sat down near the head of the bed. I looked up at Grace and tried to gesture toward the door.

"I need to get home and start our dinner," she said. "I'll bring a dish over for you all, too."

"Thank you," I managed to murmur.

I wanted to reach up and stroke Ginna's brown hair, but my arms were too weak to move.

"I knew it would probably do me in," I whispered, "But going shopping with you two was the best thing I could have done yesterday. It's something we'll always remember as one of the good times." Ginna made no response at first, but raised her head when I spoke again. "I knew my end was coming soon. I wanted to leave you and Annie with something special."

"Oh, Mom, you've given up so much because of me."

"No, I haven't. I've only done what any mother would. Just loved you unconditionally. The thing I want you to remember most is that I haven't earned my way to heaven. There are many mistakes I made because I'm only human. Everything we have is a gift from God. Always remember that—"

***

Ginna must have taken care of telling Danny the news, for he started coming to see me whenever he could get away from his classes. Annie began school on time the next week. I wasn't sure what Ginna told her daughter, but she seemed to understand that her grandma might not be around for Christmas this year.

Grace stopped by often, usually with some extra food. I wished there was something I could do to thank her. The visiting nurse came each morning to help me get started for the day. Once a week, she managed to get me into the shower. After a month or so, this had to change to a sponge bath. She monitored my vitals and made sure I wasn't in too much pain. This was palliative care, she told me.

Some things began to blur after fall came in late September. At times, I couldn't separate dreams from reality. All I could do was hope I wasn't being too much of a burden on my loved ones.

On a few of my more lucid days, I'd ask Grace or the nurse to read verses from my Bible. If it was evening, Ginna or Danny would do it. Often, when Annie got home from school, she sang some of our favorite songs, especially *Jesus Loves Me*.

One morning, Ginna came into my room carrying her laptop.

"I have something to show you, Mom."

I opened my eyes and murmured, "Why aren't you at work?"

"It's a Saturday."

"Oh, okay."

Ginna set the laptop in front of me, where I had a clear view of the screen. "This is something called Skype," she said. "It's a way to talk to people over the Internet, even if they're far away."

"Really? Who?"

"You'll see."

Ginna hit a couple of icons, and a man's face appeared on the screen. Behind him was a blonde woman.

"Hello, Lauren," he said. As soon as I heard his voice, I knew it was Dave. He looked older, but in many ways just as handsome as I remembered. "I'd like to introduce you to my wife, Sharon." He placed a hand on the woman's shoulder and she smiled and nodded her head.

"We've been married about a year now," he continued. "Ginna thought you'd like to know that Sharon has taken the seed you planted and helped it grow."

"Seed?" I managed to clear my mind enough to understand what he was saying.

"Yes, the seed of faith. Remember what you told me that morning in Spokane? Back then I felt so self-sufficient. When my wife and I eventually divorced, I realized I did need something more. Then, God sent Sharon to help me find Him."

"Actually, God searches out and finds us," his wife said.

"Yes, He does," I managed to add.

"For some reason, Ginna looked me up on the Internet, and once she told me about your illness, I knew I had to tell you this."

I glanced over at my daughter, who smiled. "You can find almost anyone on Google, Mom. I wasn't sure at first why I did it, but I guess it was God's leading, because Dave had been wanting to share this with you."

"Yes," he said. "I'm so sorry to hear about the cancer, Lauren."

"Please, don't be," I murmured. "I'll be in a beautiful place soon, with no more tears or pain."

"I remember what you said to me the last time we were together," he added. "About hoping you'd see me in heaven. Now I can assure you that you will."

Tears were flooding my face, but I was too weak to wipe them. "I'll be watching for you, Dave. And you, too, Sharon. God moves in mysterious ways."

I closed my eyes and sank into a warm, peaceful sleep.

***

Strange sounds echoed in my head. Was I dead? I saw only darkness until a green glimmer of light appeared in front of me. Then I heard the sound of voices. Maybe I was still in my bedroom, after all.

One of the voices moved nearer, and the light grew stronger. Was someone saying my name?

"L-lau-r-ren." It resonated like waves on a shore, or an echo coming back across a mountain valley.

I'm ready, Lord. I wanted to say this aloud, but found no voice of my own.

A hand touched my cheek, and another rested on my shoulder.

Dave, is that you? Again the words were only in my mind.

"You know my name as Emmanuel, Lauren. I've always been with you. It's what my name means. Even when you wandered away like a wayward sheep, I sought you out and brought you back. I healed your pain as much as you let me. For you've always been my beloved child, and now you are coming to dwell in the place I've prepared for you.

"Do not fear for your children. Ginna and Danny will be cared for. Their descendants as well. Everything will be corrected when the time is right. All things come to those who wait."

Those words. Where have I heard something like this before? Yes, my own mother. It was the last thing she said before she died:

"…those who wait upon the Lord will renew their strength … and will rise up on wings like eagles…"

Even as these words filled my mind, I began rising, supported by nothing–lifted, as though I now had wings of my own.

EPILOGUE

Our mother died in early October of 2015. Danny, Sandy, and Annie were with me keeping watch the last few hours. She'd been in and out of consciousness, but never very lucid. The only times Mom seemed to know we were there was when we sang her favorite hymns.

The last time I saw her open her eyes, she exclaimed, "Oh, it's so beautiful, Ginna!"

Mom's face was filled with wonder. Then her whole body relaxed, and she went back into unconsciousness. I waited a long time, holding her hand. At last, I just had to move and gave my chair to Annie.

When I came back from going to the bathroom, I could see Mom was dead. Her face was calm, her eyes were closed, and yet something was missing. Her life force was gone.

Annie looked up at me and said, "She died, didn't she?"

I held my daughter close. "Yes, she's gone to heaven."

Tears were soaking my shirt where Annie's face touched it. "She promised to watch for me at the gates, Mommy."

"Did she say that today?"

Annie shook her head. "It was last summer when we were sitting in the sun on the porch."

"Don't worry, Honey. I know it's true. We will see her again someday, where there's no more cancer or pain. The Bible says Jesus will wipe all the tears from our eyes."

OPTIONAL BONUS PAGES

"More of the Story: Through Ginna's Eyes"

Based on *The Peaks Saga*, Book 4,
"When the World Grows Cold"

I woke slowly. The aching in my joints reminded me that I was in my forties now. Where had all the time gone?

The first time the GAP-crossers came for Danny and me, I was only thirteen. With their help we crossed space and time to see their lives in the distant future of the Thirty-first Century. What we learned gave us courage to face the changes brought by our parents' divorce and the move from our Texas home to small-town Eastern Colorado.

When they brought us back, it was a shock to learn no time had passed in our own Twenty-first Century. We'd returned to our little house in Deer Path, Colorado on the same night we left.

As I went into high school, I began to tell myself it had all been just a dream or an illusion. Things like that couldn't really happen, could they? Then to my shock, when I was almost seventeen, Jon and Jael, these GAP-crossers, came back.

This time, Jon told us he could merge our lives with Jael and his sister Martina, because we were forerunners of them, living in a parallel universe. I was skeptical. No, I was terrified at first. What would it be like to merge minds with someone else? A stranger, in fact? Would my own self be lost? Or would I feel like a person with a split personality? Yet, I went along, for Martina had come with them, and I could see something in her eyes that told me this was meant to be.

Neither of my speculations were an accurate description of what I experienced while I was 'within' Martina. I could see what she saw, think her thoughts. Yet there were still thoughts of my own that sometimes bubbled to the surface of my awareness. At times, we were even able to communicate with each other, like telepathy, I suppose.

The strangest part was how I began to feel exactly what she felt, happiness, fear, even love. When Jon crashed their space ship, I was paralyzed with fear. For a time it looked like Martina would be the only survivor, and all her fears flowed through me. I couldn't bear to lose the dearest people in my life, my brother, and my lover. Yes, Martina was beginning to realize she did love Jon, and as a result, I was attracted to him, too.

When Jon and Jael finally healed from their injuries, and we found our way to Earth, Martina and Jon became partners and eventually married. This is where things got complicated for me. I was 'really there' with Jon, in the same way Martina was. He became my mate, too, in my own psyche.

Then, for some reason, Martina became attracted to a co-worker named Garek, and had a brief affair with him. I was there, too, of course. Again confusion filled me. Martina was no virgin, and she'd been with several men during her time in the Wilds of their home planet, Terres. But I had no such experiences. In my mind, I was still a virgin.

I began to wonder if my emotional attraction to Garek, and especially to Jon, were because I hadn't made love to any man before 'entering' Martina's mind. She was used to thinking of men as playthings, but I wasn't.

When Jon brought us back through the GAP, no time had passed in our own world, just like the first time. I was still almost seventeen and soon to be a senior in high school. Because of the mind-merging experiment, this second return was much more difficult for me. Danny was fond of Jael and missed him for a long time, but for me it felt as if a part of myself had been ripped away.

I'd been there intimately as Martina went through her choices between Garek and Jon, including when she'd made love with each of them. I was still 'within' her during her pregnancy, wondering for nine months whose child this was. Her daughter was born with brown eyes, like Jon's. Garek had the recessive blue eyes, so this question was answered. Celestia was Jon's daughter.

Then back in my own time, I discovered I was pregnant. In total confusion, I couldn't even believe it at first. How could this have happened? Did I somehow get pregnant when Martina did, but mine was delayed until I was back in my own body? It all seemed impossible.

There was no denying what my body was telling me, though. Despite my attempts to hide it, Mom noticed.

She sat me down on the couch one day and confronted me. "I know you're pregnant, Ginna. Who's the father?"

I shook my head and tried to think, but there was no answer. "I don't know."

"Why not?" she snapped. "How many men have you slept with?"

"In this century, none," was all I could say.

"What is that supposed to mean?"

I tried to explain the GAP-crossers to her, but she didn't believe me. Tears filled my eyes.

Suddenly, she pulled me into a hug. "Are you trying to tell me someone raped you?"

I just nodded. There was nothing else I could do. I didn't know myself exactly what had happened. I was so frightened and confused that all I could do was sob.

"Cry, if it helps." She stroked my hair. "I'm here for you, Honey. Whatever I can do to help, we'll work this out."

In many ways, we did get closer then, for she supported me through the pregnancy and Annie's early years. I knew she was having an affair, and when she told me the truth about my dad, I could see why. She couldn't go on bearing that pain alone.

Besides, who was I to judge her? After all, I was the unwed mother, though I was still confused about how it happened. I had no idea who Annie's father was, though I wondered if it could be Garek or Jon. There was no way to find out because I'd never see either of them again.

With Mom and my brother Danny's help we made it through the first years of my baby's infancy and toddlerhood. Then Mom found the lump in her breast. We were all devastated. At least Annie got to know her before she died, because she battled the cancer for four years.

She also made sure Danny and I got the house. With only a high school education, there weren't many jobs open to me, and we were in a rural area. The law office I'd worked at in Greeley moved to Denver. I couldn't afford to move, so I worked what other jobs I could find, including waitressing in the evening. Eventually, I managed to land a day job as a receptionist at the power plant where Mom had worked. Someone there probably hired me for Mom's sake, but I never knew who it was.

Danny did his best to help, but I wouldn't let him drop out of college at Greeley. By the time he graduated in agribusiness, he and Sandy were hoping to start a family of their own. He never asked me to pay my half of the house payments, and I knew he took the job at the feed store in Sterling so he could stay close to us. I'm sure he'd gotten better offers in faraway places.

As Annie grew, her love for music became more and more obvious. When I bought her a guitar, she was thrilled and taught herself to play it. Listening to her playing and singing reminded me of Martina's brother Darien from that other universe. He'd played an instrument called the Manitar, and I remembered Martina had played the flute.

Somewhere in my memories, I thought Garek had said his daughter was a talented musician. (Strange to call events in the future memories, but in my mind they were.) With Annie's eyes turning to bright blue as she grew, and her talent for music, my mind began to wonder if Garek might be her father.

Many a night, I tossed and turned, wondering if it was even possible. This was beyond my comprehension, and there was no one I dared explain it to. Perhaps I could have talked to Danny, but I didn't want to interfere in his life. I'd tried to tell Mom, but she never believed me, and I finally gave up. No one but me ever knew my thoughts about Annie.

Things seemed to go well for my daughter up through high school. I knew some of the kids in town talked behind her back about her being fatherless. I tried to share how Danny and

I coped with been bullied in school, when we first came here. I was thankful when she began turning to God for strength, and developed a close relationship with David, our pastor's son.

But fate turned against me. David left her with a promise ring when he went away to college, but I couldn't afford to send Annie. Perhaps this was one reason she became so angry and rebellious. Packing her guitar and little else, she moved to Denver to play in bars, hoping to start a career in music. She and David had a falling out which I didn't understand. I knew they'd been too young to marry, but part of me wished they had. Maybe things would have gone better.

For years, Annie cut me off. Weeks, even months would go by without a word. She wandered up and down the West Coast, I think. I told myself this was something she had to work through, as she tried to find her place in a world which seemed against her from the start. I hoped she didn't know she was breaking my heart.

Then the strangest thing happened. She turned up in my driveway in a rental car, with a girl who looked like Martina. This was Martina's daughter, Celestia, born 25 years before, and she brought my daughter back to me. For the first time in ages, one of my prayers had been answered.

ABOUT THE AUTHOR

M.F. (Mary Frances) Erler is a music teacher, outdoor educator, and author of fantasy fiction and non-fiction. Her teaching career has spanned over 30 years, and she has been writing most of her life. Her first Christian-based science-fiction book, *"The Peaks at the Edge of the World"* was re-written and revised in 2017, followed by six other books in the series.

Erler has been writing most of her life. In fact, some of the characters in *The Peaks Saga* were initially conceived in her youth. Her lifelong goal has been to bring spiritual ideas into fantasy-fiction, in the spirit of writers like J.R.R. Tolkien and C.S. Lewis. She enjoys public speaking and sharing her faith journey. She is an approved speaker for Women's Connections, a Stonecroft Ministry.

Now that she has published *The Peaks Saga,* she is embarking on a new venture in fiction, first with *"Voices in the Past,"* a historical fiction, and now *"Lauren's Dark Passage,"* which is contemporary fiction. These books are stand-alones, not part of a series, like the Peaks books.

Her books are designed to appeal to young adults and all who are young at heart. Among her many hobbies, Erler especially enjoys travel. She has been to several countries, including China, New Zealand, the British Isles, and Western Europe, as well as Canada, Mexico, Jamaica, and 45 of the 50

States. Her favorite mode of travel is cruising, but her current favorite place is her home in Montana.

Along with fantasy, true science, and science fiction, she is also a student of history, comparative religion, ecology, and music. Previous publications include non-fiction articles in *Today's Christian Parent,* and *Social Studies and the Young Learner,* as well as poems and short sketches in Standard Publishing Program Books. In addition, she has produced *Music in God's World,* a music curriculum for preschools, and *Wonders of Creation, an Environmental Education Curricula* for use in schools and camp settings. She has worked as a newspaper reporter and columnist, and was writer for various U.S. Forest Service publications, including being in charge of producing the book, *Targhee Lodgepole-Tragedy or Opportunity?*

She has a Bachelor of Science in Environmental Education and Biology from Colorado State University, and a Masters of Music Education from Concordia University-Chicago. In her senior year of high school, she was awarded a prize for her writing by the National Council of Teachers of English, the Quill and Scroll Award for Journalism, and a National Merit Scholarship.

Her love of singing has led to participation in many choirs and acapella groups, which enabled her to perform at two International Sweet Adelines conventions in Nashville and Houston. She sang with these women's barbershop groups for 18 years. Hobbies include reading, singing, playing several musical instruments, and acrylic painting. She and her husband, Paul, have two adult children who are also teachers. All make their home in the northwest. You are invited to connect with her at mferler@peaksandbeyond.com or on her blog at MFErler.blogspot.com.